THE BIG BET

Checkmate

Owen B. Greenwald

EPIC
Press

Checkmate
The Big Bet: Book #6

Written by Owen B. Greenwald

Copyright © 2016 by Abdo Consulting Group, Inc.

Published by EPIC Press™
PO Box 398166
Minneapolis, MN 55439

Cover design by Candice Keimig
Images for cover art obtained from iStockPhoto.com
Edited by Ryan Hume

LIBRARY OF CONGRESS CATALOGING-IN-PUBLICATION DATA

Greenwald, Owen B.
Checkmate / Owen B. Greenwald.
p. cm. — (The big bet ; #6)
Summary: No more games—the Mafia wants Jason and his team dead, and it wants
them dead yesterday. Jason and the others can see only one way out: to fake their
deaths and flee the country. Is this the end of Jason's story? Will this be the end of
his life?
ISBN 978-1-68076-188-7 (hardcover)
1. Swindlers and swindling—Fiction. 2. Deception—Fiction.
3. Young adult fiction. I. Title.
[Fic]—dc23
2015949062

EPIC
Press

EPICPRESS.COM

For the three who mattered most,
who were my beginning,
and, so help me, will be my end.
You made all things possible.

ONE

OWE YOU AN APOLOGY.

I wasn't truthful with you from the beginning, about how this story ends. That's how I am—when I tell stories, I string my audience along. Keeps me in the spotlight longer.

Well, we're at the end. Not the very end, but close enough. And not the end for *forever*, mind—life goes on after the credits roll.

For some of us.

Hopefully, it'll be clear why this particular story ends where it does. And again, I'm not gonna ruin it for you, because that'd spoil the experience. Also because some things I literally *can't* say.

But endings are really just beginnings in disguise, when you think about it. One thing ends, another begins. Very zen.

That much, I can promise you. There's not just an ending coming, but a beginning too.

In a way, this entire story was the beginning. I wish I'd known that while it was happening— maybe I could've fucked up a little less along the way. At least you get the *warning*. And while I can't reveal what comes next, that's just because for once, I dunno either. Could be anything.

Maybe I'll tell you when I find out. If I can.

You probably thought you were getting a complete story, not the very beginning . . . but that's not why I'm apologizing. You should've seen that coming when you grabbed a book about teenagers. That's what the teen years *are*—the beginning of the rest of your life. Your chance to set the foundations of a truly epic story. And that's just what we did.

Not that those teenage years can't be epic in their own right. I can't imagine I'll ever face off against a more odious weasel than Richard Trieze, or be more terrified than I was the first time someone held me at gunpoint, or dream as big as I did in the CPC. It's funny how *fast* that last year went—all the events jumble together into a mess, with just those few crisp, vivid memories standing out. I don't think I could ever forget them no matter *what* my future holds, even if the rest of my adolescence fades into the mist.

Addie, too, I don't think I'll forget. You *never* forget your first love, or so they say. She was technically my second, but that doesn't lessen my feelings even slightly.

I never told her I loved her . . . out of confusion over my own feelings, or some misguided fear she wouldn't take it well. It was hard even admitting it to myself, honestly. Lucas fucked up my idea of love pretty badly—it's one of the dozen-odd things I'll never forgive him for. Not even on his deathbed. Or mine.

So the story itself's important. It *matters*. I don't

wanna downplay that just because it doesn't end on the final concluding moment of my life—and if it did, I couldn't have told it. I haven't gotten there yet.

I said I owed you an apology, and I've been tiptoeing around it. That's not like me.

I'm sorry.

Sorry I didn't make it clear from the start this story doesn't end happily. I know sad endings really bring some people down. If that describes you, just pretend the story ended right where I stopped before, with the gang driving triumphantly out of Lorenzo Michaelis's trap, leaving him and his goons to be arrested. That seems a happy enough note to end on.

But then, it gets bad. Real bad. Bad enough I figured I owed you some warning up front, seeing as you've stuck with me this long.

Not gonna say more than that—except that again, this is truly the end.

The end of the beginning.

TWO

OUR HEADLIGHTS SCYTHED THROUGH THE NIGHT ahead, illuminating the expanse of highway as it vanished beneath us.

Kira was driving as fast as she dared. The cop locator app was open on her iPhone, which she'd propped up on the dashboard. We adopted more socially-acceptable speeds whenever a police car got too close, but never for too long. Kira herself had been uncharacteristically silent during the drive, only occasionally speaking up to report our progress. Maybe she was finally feeling her injuries.

Absent Kira, the rest of us'd fallen mostly silent

too. We were turned inward, thinking through the repercussions of the last few hours.

We'd just gotten the street boss of the Bonanno family arrested. In theory, anyway—Lorenzo had escaped a similar trap before, and had doubtless survived countless others over the course of his rise to power. But success or failure, the attempt was unlikely to have made us many friends.

They'd be coming for us.

It hadn't been dark when we left the Catskills, but it'd darkened noticeably since then. As the sun'd sank towards the horizon, I'd seen it as the embodiment of time passing, running out. The Mafia would *not* need this long to arrange a retributive strike. They knew where we'd be coming from and where we were going. The faster we moved, the less time they'd have, but . . . it was a *long* drive back from the Catskills. Probably one of the reasons Lorenzo'd picked it as the meeting spot. And Kira could drive as fast as she liked, but we were still beholden to the laws of physics, and there's just no *way* we could all get home before the Mafia could organize, not in the age of instantaneous electronic communication.

My GPS displayed the estimated remaining travel time as thirty-nine minutes. Too long.

We seemed to be slowing again. I looked at the locator app expecting to see a cop warning, but then I realized Kira was shifting into an exit lane.

"What's happening?" I asked.

Kira kept her eyes on the road as she answered, a rarity for her. "Almost outta gas."

I craned my neck. Sure enough, the needle indicator was pushing up against empty.

"Fucking shit," I muttered. We didn't have time for this.

But I knew—as we all did—that if we didn't have time to stop, we certainly didn't have time to run out of gas and wait, stranded, for AAA.

We pulled into the closest gas station, a Chevron that cheerily advertised the presence of Quiznos sandwiches inside. Z, who'd called dibs on the bathroom, got out before the car'd even stopped moving and broke into a run for the door.

"Food," I said to Addie, and she gave an affirmative reply. I hadn't been letting us stop for food before (we'd made a single stop early on to retrieve the seven million dollars we'd stashed at Claryville—*that* risk/reward judgment'd been easily defensible), but I wasn't gonna waste the opportunity if we had to anyway.

Addie and Kira got out, and I followed their lead. Even if I didn't have an assigned task, stretching felt good. Above me, the neon glare of the Chevron logo advertised the station's existence far and wide.

We were too exposed here. It was ridiculous to imagine the Mafia'd have a reason to check this particular gas station, but if they *did* . . .

Suddenly feeling foolish for indulging the need to stretch, I ducked behind a car door and motioned Kira—who was pumping gas—to do the same. She looked skeptical, but came anyway. She was very obviously trying to hide a limp, but not quite succeeding.

"What?"

"I'm giving you marching orders," I said. "Who knows what we'll find in the city. Derek's teams're skeleton crews until the main team returns from the Catskills, so your homes are vulnerable. We're gonna park in a garage and send Addie to scout and gather info. I need you to watch her back, if you're up to it."

"Of course I'm up to it."

"You sure? You've been pretty quiet this—"

"I'm *up to it*," growled Kira with a touch of the old anger. I grinned, satisfied. I wasn't happy about whatever monster she was becoming, but right now, I *needed* that monster. And I'd use it in whatever capacity I could to save us.

"The job's yours, then. I'd ask Z to tap his mob contacts, but I have a feeling they'll be more liability than asset right now."

"Probs."

Z got back a little later and passed the key to Kira, who had second dibs (which I'm still not convinced is a thing). With the key came a warning about the state of the room, which did nothing to dissuade Kira—in fact, she looked almost eager. As she strolled towards the bathroom, I turned to Z.

"Ready for your marching orders?"

"Sure."

"We need somewhere to stay for a bit," I said. "Not one of our houses, not my apartment."

It would've made the most sense to use Lucas's place. Its security was tight—almost doubled since the attack a few months ago—and there was plenty of room. But there was no way Lucas would let us use the place, and no way I'd ask him.

Forget the possibility that he was actively moving against me. Even in the *best case scenario*, I couldn't see that working out. I'd be willing to shelve my pride and ask if there was even the smallest *chance* he'd say yes, but why waste time? I could picture him meeting us in the entrance hall, staring down from his height of six-foot-two with an amused smile, asking why we'd thought he'd take kindly to us bringing our problems to his doorstep *again* (he hadn't been happy about the last assassination attempt). Then he'd wave a massive palm at one of his several security details with a single cocked eyebrow that signaled he'd be *much* happier if we were removed from the premises. And that'd be that. Even if a team of hit men were waiting on his front porch.

No, the mansion I'd grown up in was not an option.

"They'll be watching the hotels," I continued. "Not all of them, but enough that I don't wanna risk it. Staying with a friend should be safe. Only I'm kinda short on friends lately."

"Can't imagine why."

I ignored him. "You've gotta know someone you could trust with your life, who'd be happy hosting some strangers for a few days, wouldn't ask too many questions, and also isn't immediately associable with you."

Z gave me a sharp look. "A few days?"

"At most," I said, avoiding his gaze. "I wanna be prepared for the worst-case scenario."

What I didn't say was that we'd hopefully be on a plane to Europe by then, because I'd already brought up the need to leave New York forever and been mostly shut down. None of the others really understood what we were up against—that once the mob's gloves came off, there wasn't much we could do besides place ourselves in protective custody . . . or go somewhere far away. Everyone but me had ties to the area, and they'd be making their decisions based on that. At least I could rely on Addie to see the necessity of leaving, even if she'd mourn her decision.

Hopefully *she* could bring the other two around, because *I* didn't have time to—I'd be busy organizing our flights out and making sure our families'd be safe. Attacking them'd been a costly operation for the Bonannos last time, but I couldn't rely on fear keeping them away. Nor was I sure whether their code of honor kept them from explicitly targeting our families.

This whole mess was Z's fault, but I was pretty sure he knew that, so I was trying to avoid saying it. It made for an awkward silence, the two of us crouched behind the car door, listening to the gas flow and watching the numbers on the meter climb. Kira's return from the bathroom couldn't come soon enough.

She came back smirking and winked, gesturing behind her. "Have fun in there."

I felt a surge of foreboding—Kira's smirks rarely heralded something fun—but I *did* really need to go, so what choice was there?

The stench of the bathroom leaked through the door and I almost turned back, but taking the time to find a different one could have disastrous consequences, and I certainly wasn't holding it in. I turned away from the door, took a deep breath, then turned the key and stepped in before I could change my mind.

There, in the corner by the toilet, was a pile of literal shit.

Not a large one—just a small pile, like someone'd squatted down and not bothered to check if he was in the right place.

It took effort to tear my eyes away from the pile and back to the bowl. It was just too perfect a physical manifestation of our current situation, which I found almost amusing enough to blot out the sheer horror of its existence.

Few places on Earth reveal the nature of humanity like a public restroom. Needless to say, I finished up as quickly as possible.

Addie was waiting by the car when I got back. She carried a bag from which emerged all sorts of aromas; they mingled together and formed a general "food" smell, and my gurgling belly decided it was the greatest smell I'd ever come across, especially compared to what I'd just put it through. Seeing me approach, she handed Z the bag and started towards the room herself. I tossed her the keys and she caught them out of the air.

"How was it?" said Z, and I made a face at him.

Kira was screwing the gas cap back on. "We're set to go when Addie gets back."

Barely seconds had passed before a grimacing Addie was climbing into the car, promising she could hold it in. None of us could blame her.

We passed our sandwiches around as Kira steered the red Civic back onto the street. The time we'd spent on that pit stop had me on edge. I wasn't even worried about anything concrete, but Lucas'd always been clear about the folly of giving your enemies too much time. *Time, like anything else, is a resource. You wouldn't hand a rival the contents of your wallet, so why give them more time than the absolute minimum?*

To blot out his obnoxious voice, I bit into my sandwich—ham and Swiss with tomato and peppers. It was pretty terrible, especially given my usual standards, but it took the edge off my hunger and, as a bonus, gave me a sterling excuse to stay quiet while I thought. Can't ask for more than that.

The sandwiches lasted us another twenty minutes, long enough that I was now recognizing familiar landmarks—the network of creeks off the Hackensack River, and just past it, the Walmart. Little signs of home, calming me in spite of myself.

"Making good time," said Kira, still in that strangely subdued voice. "No traffic, so that's nice."

She was right, I realized, as I looked out the window. The highway was practically deserted. Not that it was usually crowded this time of night—rush hour was long past—but the road ahead should've been heavily speckled with taillights this close to the city. There were some, sure, but not many.

On a whim, I glanced back towards the mountains. Again, there were some headlights coming our direction, but they were few and far away, with the exception of one car that was making to pass on our left.

And (this is embarrassing to admit) I thought for a moment—just a moment—what a sinister-looking dark van it was. Didn't assign any significance to its clichéd appearance whatsoever.

Only for a moment, I again must clarify. Then it hit me—the realization, not the car.

And in that same moment, the car drew level with us and their side door began to open . . .

"Kira, step on it!"

Delivered with that much urgency behind it, there was no excuse for disobeying, or even questioning. There was only that moment, and Kira's "stepping on it" was of paramount importance to us getting *more* moments.

She did, giving the car a great rush of power as the black van's door slid open fully.

The engine roared in protest, but we surged forward. As we did, the sound of gunfire split the air.

THREE

F YOU HEARD THE BULLET, IT DIDN'T KILL YOU. That was one of old Lucas's favorites. For some reason, I'd always taken that metaphorically. Now I understood. Understood that the shock of the gunshot could paralyze you for a few critical seconds as you tried to figure out if you were dead or not. Much simpler to remember that aphorism and keep moving, or the second shot'd do what the first hadn't.

I made that mistake. Kira didn't.

"Heads down!" she barked, but the words didn't register immediately and it was only when Addie repeated the order that I ducked my head below the rear windshield. This made it much harder to see what was going on, but that seemed a fair trade for the decreased chance of becoming a fatality.

The car shuddered beneath me as Kira pushed it to its limit. There were more shots, each as loud as their predecessors, but she sat straight and tall in the driver's seat, utterly unafraid. Though I couldn't see it, I could picture her grimace of concentration.

She's absolutely crazy and probably a menace to society. And lately, I've been flat-out uncomfortable having her on the team, no matter the advantage she brings. But situations like this remind me why I keep her around.

Tires squealed, and I had to actively fight the urge to peek my head up. Instead, I reached out and took Addie's hand. She squeezed so tight her nails dug into my skin, but I didn't mind. The pain was another sign I was still alive.

The shock of the situation'd worn off, though, and the part of my brain that was shitting itself in terror'd been cordoned off in favor of the part that looked at the chaotic mess of life and charted a path through it to success. Already, my breathing was slowing, becoming even.

Assets . . . precious few. Restrictions . . . a whole shitload.

"Got a plan up front?" I asked, trying to project calmness.

"Don't get hit," said Kira.

"Awesome. Anything more specific?"

More screeching. Kira growled in frustration.

"I'm doing my best, 'kay? It's not as easy as it looks."

So it was up to me.

If *I* were the Mafia, what would my plan be, and how could my targets best foil it . . . ?

"Kira," I said urgently. "We need to get off the highway. Our direction's too predictable right now."

Kira grunted. The car swayed like a drunkard and Addie and I gripped each other tighter.

"If I'd organized this, I'd have put more cars in Lincoln tunnel. Dark, enclosed, great for an ambush. There's more there, I know it."

"Weehawken okay?"

I didn't see why not. If we could navigate through it to Holland Tunnel, we could make it through to Manhattan . . . provided they didn't have people stationed *there* too. And while the NYPD was likely compromised, I couldn't see the mob placing as high a value on *Weehawken* police.

"You can't see out the back window anymore," reported Z. "And our right mirror's shot off."

We wouldn't last much longer. The shots'd continued without pause from the van behind us, and only luck mixed with Kira's erratic weaving'd kept them from hitting anything important. But if we didn't do something soon . . .

"Kira—"

"I'm *on it.*"

My brain was still running through options, listing equipment on hand, favors owed, *anything* that could tip the scales in our favor. Derek and his team? But they'd been wrapping up in the Catskills when we left, and almost certainly were driving slower than Kira. They wouldn't be nearby.

The reserves we'd left guarding our houses were closer, but calling on them would leave our families undefended. That could be the purpose of this attack—to draw them away. I couldn't take that risk in good conscience.

No, we were on our own.

What I *should've* done was abandon the Civic in Claryville and pick up a car the Mafia wouldn't recognize. We had enough money in the trunk to straight-up *buy* a new car, no questions asked. It was a foolish mistake, an amateurish mistake, but I hadn't been paranoid enough. You can *never* be paranoid enough.

But flagellating myself for my past error wouldn't save us now. I needed to focus on getting the details right *this* time. Back down the list of assets . . .

The car *jerked* to the right, hard. I shouted,

more from surprise than fear, and the hammer-like gunshots died away briefly. This was followed by a crash and then the car started bouncing as if traveling through rough terrain.

"One guardrail down," said Kira calmly. "One to go."

Guardrail?

There was a second crash, followed by Kira's steady, "We're through."

"Through *what?*"

Kira didn't answer, spinning the wheel expertly. I heard a loud, irate honk, which abruptly cut off as more bullets rattled the car. I felt something pass over my head, and sank another couple inches into the seat. When I lifted my eyes, I saw that cracks'd formed around a bullet embedded in the windshield. On our side of the glass.

Behind me, just inches above my head, was a small hole that definitely hadn't been there earlier.

I took a deep, calming breath, trying to reconcile myself with my imminent death . . . and couldn't.

It was hard enough just keeping the mania at bay, not indulging my urge to start screaming and never stop. Addie's hand was like a vice on mine. I tried to squeeze it reassuringly, but I was already squeezing as tightly as I could.

Then the car made such a sharp turn I swear two of its wheels left the ground. The lurch threw me into the door and Addie bounced against her seatbelt. The gunfire stopped again, though, leaving a pleasant sort of relative silence.

"Nice," said Z, at the same time Kira said, "Fucking Christshit on a dick sandwich."

"Another van," she explained, still driving at almost twice the urban speed limit, "tried to cut me off. Made it onto a cross street in time, but I dunno if"—a sudden chorus of honking car horns—"there's a good way to the tunnel from here. Just hang tight."

Like we had a choice.

Over the honking and the engines and the bullets, I heard the shrill alarm of multiple police sirens, discordant with each other, getting steadily louder, and allowed myself a sigh of relief. Corruption in the police or no, there's no way they could let this slide—or fail to do anything but their utmost to rescue us.

"Towards the sirens," I ordered. Kira didn't respond. She looked like an electric fence—utterly motionless, but struck through with dangerous levels of energy—and her focus was absolute, not to be disturbed for words unless vitally important.

This was a woman—not a girl, not anymore— who, less than a week ago, should've by all rights been dead—and was still taking a mix of painkillers just to be functional. But no hint of that showed in her posture. She looked no less composed than a Shaolin monk seeking enlightenment (then again, a combination gunfight/car chase probably *was* Kira's personal ideal of enlightenment).

"GPS me Holland tunnel," she said to Z, who began typing almost robotically into his phone.

I did my best to determine what the various

cars were doing based on the way ours moved, but it was almost impossible. It was *frustrating*, more than anything—being jerked around by physics while curled into a ball on a car floor, having no idea what was going on, holding tight to my girl-friend as if she was the last secure thing on this planet.

One thing I *could* track without sight was the sirens. I listened to them drawing closer and closer, hoping with every fiber of my being that they'd arrive before a lucky shot found its mark. Finally, I had to accept that they weren't actually getting louder anymore. In fact—though I tried to deny the obvious as long as possible—they seemed to be getting *softer*.

"Go *towards* the police," I growled. Now was *not* the time for Kira to indulge her thrill-seeking side.

"Doing my best," she grunted. "They keep cut-ting me off. You realize I'm evading *three* vans of people trying to kill us?"

"When'd the third arrive?"

"A while ago," said Kira. "It's really fucking me up. I should've said something."

If the Mafia could afford to field three vans in *Weehawken*, they probably could've arranged a distraction for the police, enough that perhaps their converging on *our* position'd be delayed several crucial minutes—which may not seem like much, but on death-race-car-gun time, a few minutes is *eons*.

It came to me then. The way out. Well, *a* way out. But just thinking it made me feel dirty, so I sure as hell wasn't gonna tell the others. Not unless things got *really* desperate . . .

But then, things were really desperate *now*. If I was putting off sharing the plan until they got *more* desperate, then by induction, I wouldn't tell anyone until we were all four shot to death.

I opened my mouth, but I was interrupted by a ferocious crunch and everything got darker. But the car seemed functional, and we were all still breathing, so what could've—

Desperately, *foolishly*, I whipped my head up and looked out the window just in time to see what looked like a furnished *living room* before we crashed through a large front window onto a lawn.

I ducked back down, curiosity fully sated—and a little lightheaded. "Did you just crash us through a *house?*"

No reply. Kira was radiating fierce determination now, the same determination she sometimes displayed when crunching a particularly difficult computer problem. In this state, she became almost unresponsive, especially when I was asking a question she knew I already could answer for myself.

Just how durable *were* Civics, anyway? We were probably rapidly approaching the point where the car would simply stop working.

"Shit," said Z suddenly, making eye contact with me from where he lay huddled in the front seat. "I forgot—"

But rather than elaborating on what he'd forgotten, he reached a short-fingered hand up to the glove box, opened it with a *click,* and drew out a small handgun. As soon as I saw it, I wanted to hang myself in shame for forgetting—it was the gun he'd taken from the *valchiria.*

It wasn't much—one gun against at least eight. But it was something.

"Of *course*," I breathed. "Good thinking. Okay, who's the best marksman?"

General consensus was Kira. Addie was quick to point out that she couldn't drive *and* shoot—not only was it logistically impractical, there was probably a law against it. If you couldn't drive while *texting*, driving while discharging firearms was probably right out. And if it wasn't, it really *should* be.

"I used to go to the range with Dad sometimes," said Z slowly. "Y'know, before he . . . Well, I wasn't too bad."

"You good with this?" I asked him. I wasn't

sure whether I meant *shooting at people* or *stepping into the line of fire for us.* Maybe both. I dunno which way he took it, but he nodded. There was a grim set to his jaw.

"Then show them we can shoot back."

Z gave me a determined grin that utterly failed to mask his fear, then started rolling down his window.

"Coordinate with him, Kira."

Kira again gave no indication she'd heard, but at some point in the twisting, squealing madness she said, still placid, "One open."

Z lifted himself, sighted along the barrel, and fired. He shrugged as he dropped back down. "Dunno if I hit. Can't tell either way."

I could still hear sirens, but at this point, I had to accept that they weren't concerned with us right now. If the Mafia was really tying up the whole of Weehawken's police force, this operation represented a monumental use of resources. Someone *really* wanted us dead.

My mind flashed to Richard—but no, we'd . . . Well, he wasn't around anymore. I'd seen the obit. If Lorenzo'd escaped the trap we'd laid in the mountains, it was likely him, throwing his full weight against us with a vengeance. Or, I realized with a sudden chill, Lucas could finally be making his move. He definitely had the resources for an operation of this scale, and as for motive—

Everything was suddenly motion and noise. The Civic was spinning out of control; Kira let out an anguished shout as she lost her meditative trance, and shots were flying, hitting windows, tearing through car doors, and Z was shooting back wildly, unsure where to aim—but we were steadying, gaining speed, escaping whatever death-trap we'd found ourselves in.

"The fuck was that?" I said.

Kira's response was anything but glacially calm.

"Rammed in the ass by a fourth bitch-lifting van! Came right the fuck out of nowhere, a side street. Good thing it just clipped us . . . "

Kira's voice faded to nothing in my ear as I realized how still and silent Z'd become.

He was slumped backwards in his seat, still holding the gun. Blood was dripping down his arm, along the barrel.

"*Z!*" I shouted, and Addie stiffened at the sudden noise. She hadn't noticed either.

Hearing the shout, Z's eyes opened weakly, and my heart exploded with relief.

"I think they got me," he said, and he coughed. There was blood mixed with the cough too.

Addie was already climbing over the drink holders into the front seat, unheeding of her own safety. "Show me where it hit you, Z. Don't close your eyes."

She was bleeding too, I realized—from the arm. But she made no mention of it as she prodded Z, probed his chest and stomach, and slapped him awake when he tried to close his eyes again.

A . . . well, I'm not sure what my relationship with Z was these days but let's go with friend, was potentially dying just a few feet from me, and I was helpless to do anything but watch while my injured girlfriend did her best to keep him alive.

And outside the car, four sable vans pursued us, sharklike, through the city night.

FOUR

"**H**OLD THIS," SAID ADDIE, HANDING ME Z'S gun.

I hefted the dark metal. It was heavier than I'd expected.

Around us, the car was shaking itself apart. Kira'd been pushing the engine and steering in ways the poor car'd never been designed for, and the odd bullet hole couldn't be helping matters. Not to mention the multiple impacts. "Just a little longer," I muttered, patting the seat. The car couldn't hear me, but it made me feel better to pretend.

Z *needed* a hospital. But leading four vans full

of gunmen to a hospital was probably infinite negative karma, and I doubted hospitals were anti-Mafia sanctuaries. It hadn't worked in *The Godfather*, after all.

"I'm good," said Z woozily. "Promise."

My plan from before was back in my head, demanding consideration. Lucas was there too, nodding in approval, saying he couldn't have come up with better. I gritted my teeth against his words, but one look at Z's limp, bleeding body told me I didn't have time to think up anything else.

"Kira. How close is the tunnel?"

Kira took a glance at the GPS, which was recalculating the route based on a location we no longer inhabited. "Not sure."

"Close?"

Kira let out a macabre chuckle. "Farther away than when we fucking started. They're herding me."

The last bit of hope within me died.

You've already lost one of your 'friends'. Must you lose another before you make the choice you should've made already? Lucas's voice was loud and mocking—not to mention extremely pessimistic about Z's chance of survival.

But he was right. *Some* of us could make it out, if not all, and my hesitation was only hurting people who didn't need to be hurt.

Still not ready to make the tough decisions. If you were reluctant to abandon the money in the trunk, I'd at least understand your hesitation. This *is just embarrassing.*

"Kira," I said. She didn't respond, so I said it again, louder.

"Kira, I know you can hear me."

"That bit was tough as fuck," she said ten seconds later. "Needed to concentrate. What?"

"We're all gonna die."

"Not dead yet."

"We need to get away."

"No shit, Sherringford. *You* wanna hop in—"

"There's a way out," I said loudly, bracing myself against a particularly violent turn. "They're chasing the car. If we can lose them for a few seconds and then *abandon* the car . . . "

I let my voice trail off meaningfully. Addie, intellect that she was, grasped the implication immediately.

"To sell the illusion, the car would need to keep driving."

My silence said more than any words could've.

"Shucks," said Kira at last. "Aren't you gonna ask me to do it?"

"That's your call," I said. "I'm not—"

"Then I volunteer."

I tried to be surprised, but realized I wasn't. Of *course* Kira'd jump at the chance to play the hero and risk her life. It was what she was born to do. Maybe that was why I'd resisted putting the plan forward, knowing that the decision of who'd be sacrificed had been made the moment Kira and I first met.

It wasn't a fair decision—but life wasn't fair.

Kira must've noticed our discomfort, because

she said, "It just makes sense. I'm already driving. What're you gonna do, change drivers? It's already gonna be tough enough dumping you guys."

"I, uh." The words were stuck in my throat, or maybe they'd never formed at all. What could I even say? "Thank you" seemed inappropriate, "good luck" cavalier, even mocking.

"Weird thing is, I always figured it'd be Z who got the ultimate short straw. Guess it had to be my turn *eventually.*"

"He still might," said Addie, looking worried. "But he's safe to move, I think."

Her face was blank, showing no worry in the slightest, and I thought back to the time she'd come by my new apartment after Kira'd hit me. She'd claimed to have trouble caring about things then—was that the source of her stoicism now, or was she mourning Kira internally while putting on a brave face? Would I even be able to tell the difference if she wanted to pretend so?

"Good news," I said.

"It's not as bad as it looks, I think. I'm no doctor, but I'm reasonably confident he won't die before we can get him looked at."

"Estimate on that?"

"Ninety-five percent."

"Told you," said Z. I wondered how much of the conversation he'd picked up on. If he knew what I was asking Kira to do.

"So Kira'll shake off the pursuit a bit, get us out of their sightline. When she slows, we open the doors and jump, shut the doors, press against the walls or whatever cover we can find—it's dark, we'll be okay—and then we call a taxi and get to a hospital. Everyone clear?"

We were all clear.

The windshield was a mass of cracks at this point—it was a miracle Kira could still see out.

"Y'all be ready to go on my say," said Kira.

"I'm sorry," I said. It was the only appropriate thing I'd been able to think of.

I could hear the smile in her voice. "Why? This shit's gonna be *wicked.*"

"Brace!" she called suddenly, and something rattled the car, shoving me against the seat. As I struggled to twist myself back into position, the car floor swaying beneath me, another lurch sent me sprawling. Kira was muttering something I couldn't quite hear, but it was probably incredibly obscene.

I tried to fix these moments in my memory as best I could. Kira's bravado, her unflappability, her loyalty . . . This was Kira at her best, all her finest qualities exemplified. This was the Kira I wanted to remember at the funeral, not the rage-filled thrill addict who'd once killed a man in the ring. I owed her that much for her sacrifice.

It almost made me reconsider the entire plan. Almost.

"Can't shake them," she grunted. "Boss, can you scare them a bit?"

"Me? I can't—I mean, I've never—"

"You don't have to *hit* anything. Just get them to back off."

"Right." Okay, I could do this. Just roll down the window, point the gun, and pull the trigger. Nothing simpler. What self-respecting criminal didn't know how to use a gun, anyway? I was probably *oozing* heretofore-undiscovered natural talent.

So why was I suddenly feeling so lightheaded?

I made out something that sounded like, "Almost there . . . " from Kira. Addie motioned me to roll down my window, but the glass'd shattered and refracted beneath the force of several bullets and the window was inoperable.

"Jason, *now!*" yelled Kira.

It was now or never, whether the window was cooperating or not. I pulled the door's handle and threw my weight against it, trying not to think about how if a lucky bullet caught me, my life'd be over before I even knew what was happening. Before I could make a conscious decision, the gun in my hand was up and shooting. I stood, gripping the inside of the car for dear life, and fired until the gun clicked empty.

They were awful shots—I admit that freely. I'd been prepared for recoil, but the way the gun *jumped* in my hand was almost enough to push me onto the street, and *definitely* enough to throw off my aim completely. The shots were clean misses, every one, but they served their primary purpose— our pursuers slowed slightly, reevaluating, while Kira sped up even further.

Once it was clear no more bullets were coming out, I ducked back inside and yanked the door shut, trying to control my heart rate. My ears were ringing, and when I tapped on the door to test my hearing, I was forced to confront the fact that I was at least partially deaf for now.

I'd seen two vans behind us when I'd lifted my head to shoot. There was a third ahead now, coming up the street towards us—I could see its headlights glowing through the mass of cracks that our windshield had become. Kira sat stock still, traveling straight for the third van at ramming speed, heedless of the bullets that struck the windshield inches from her face . . . and turned sharply with seconds to spare. The van barreled past, unable to correct its path in time to follow.

The car lurched like it was being hit with a giant pendulum as Kira hit the brakes again and again. I hit the seat in front of me. Multiple times.

And then we were barely crawling forward compared to our earlier gallop and Kira was shouting again and Addie and Z were spilling out the front so I opened the door and threw myself away from the car, barely remembering to slam the door behind me, scrabbling like mad to reach a wall I could press myself against—

No, a wall was no good. I needed something to hide *behind*. There were a few doorways that offered some measure of protection and, still in don't-think mode, I made for the closest. I stuck to that door like it was flypaper and I was the world's most masochistic fly and watched as the red Civic—which was not only so battered I wasn't sure how it was still functioning, but also smoking ominously—began gathering speed again. Taking a true friend (and all our cash) with it.

Headlights illuminated the street where I'd been only moments before. I tried to press myself tighter into my alcove as two black vans drove in single file down the alleyway in hot pursuit, gunshots echoing in their wake. Through my ringing ears, they were partially muted, like I was hearing them from underwater.

Kira at least escaped the alley—when I emerged from my hiding place (after I was sure the third van wasn't immediately following the other two, and hesitantly even then), her car was gone. I imagined her, face set in determination, eyes sparkling with joy as she pushed her vehicle to its limit. Blissful to the end.

I hadn't gotten to say goodbye. Or . . . anything really, other than my pathetic "I'm sorry," which she hadn't even accepted. Everything'd happened too fast. I pulled out my phone, thinking I'd text her one last message, just so she knew how much I'd appreciated the time we'd gotten. But she wouldn't ever get the chance to read it, so what would be the point?

Instead, I dialed 911, hoping whatever was keeping the police tied up wasn't also affecting ambulances. The woman on the other end was terse but understanding, and promised someone would be on the scene shortly.

I tossed the gun, which I hadn't thought to let go of, down a storm drain. When I straightened up, Addie was standing in front of me. Her mask was cracked again, letting through a dull glint of pain.

We fell into each other's arms and held each other. I realized I was shaking, and suddenly felt like I was gonna throw up. Our group wasn't meant to be three. It just wasn't—

"She wanted it to be this way," murmured

Addie into my shoulder. "Anything less would have disappointed her."

I thought about whether this made things any better and decided it didn't. Addie didn't believe it either, I could tell. She was casting about for anything that could comfort me and throwing it out there.

"What a goddamned legend," I said, trying to make it sound like it was working, though she wouldn't be fooled for a second. We knew each other too damned well to fool each other like this. Yet we tried anyway.

"Did you hear what she said as we were getting out?" said Addie. "She looked at us as I was opening the door and gave us one of her jack-o-lantern smiles and said, 'See you bitches later.' That was the last thing I heard. It was a very . . . *Kira* thing to say, a fitting thing."

It was, I agreed. But that still didn't make it better.

I felt like I was drowning in black, cold water,

like it was all I could do to keep my head above the surface, but as I fought, my limbs grew more and more numb, and I wanted to just surrender and let the water take me.

But three members or four, this team was under my command, and until we were safe, my job wasn't over. So I divorced myself from my grief as best I could, set it aside with the intention of revisiting it when I had a chance, and stepped away from Addie towards Z where he lay on the ground, cradling his stomach.

His breathing was coming in harsh gasps and he didn't seem to be in any condition to talk. So I just sat by him and held his head in my lap until the ambulance arrived.

FIVE

THE REAL PROBLEM WITH KIRA'S GAMBIT, ASIDE from her sacrifice, was that we weren't dead.

That is, that we were *obviously* not dead. Kira's killers'd examine the car, notice they were three bodies short, and know immediately their work wasn't over. We'd still have people after us. I'd instructed Derek to remain on high alert—and in the meantime, it was probably best if we didn't go home, in case the mob was watching our houses. The best way to thwart an attack was to remove any reason for it to occur, and while I had faith in Derek's team—if I hadn't, I'd have hired someone else instead—they were a last resort. If the situation was bad enough to require them stepping in, there'd be no hiding their involvement from the families they were protecting. Explanations would be demanded . . . and probably given.

Addie and Z weren't too keen on that idea, and to Kira, such a breach in secrecy would be—well, *would've been* unthinkable.

I realized I had no idea how to break the news to Kira's parents. They'd have to be told *something*, but would Kira have cared if the truth came out after her death? She'd never told me either way— Kira'd never suspected she could die. And honestly, I hadn't either. She was *invincible*.

So put aside what Kira'd want. What'd be best from *our* perspective? Giving her grieving family the whole truth, or coming up with a tragic story?

The grief was gnawing at the corners of my consciousness again, eroding my numbness, and I squeezed my eyes shut against the rising pain of loss—contained it again, promised myself I'd give it due attention when I could afford to.

"You alright?"

I opened my eyes to see Addie looking at me with concern written all over her face—the same concern that'd suffused her question. But there was a dullness to it I didn't think she'd intended, dullness that matched the sorrow peeking out from behind her eyes.

Jersey City Medical Center's waiting room smelled *recycled* somehow. Unfortunately, it was the largest hospital within reasonable distance, meaning if anyone wanted to search nearby hospitals for their three missing targets, they'd check here first. We'd given the paramedics a false name for Z at the scene, but there was no guarantee that'd work, depending on how determined our hypothetical stalkers were. It helped that they wouldn't know *who* exactly they were looking for, or if we were even here at all—and Z was hardly the only new patient with a bullet injury tonight. Ideally, we wouldn't stay . . . but I didn't trust Z to stay alive the way I'd trusted Kira just a few days ago.

I'd *trusted* her.

"I'm okay," I said. A lie.

The paramedics hadn't even let us ride with him, much less suggest where he be taken. They'd insisted on Jersey City, reasoning—not incorrectly—that a large hospital'd be best equipped to handle his injuries. We could hardly contradict them without sounding completely crazy. Your average EMT isn't trained to deal with organized crime syndicates.

Stomach wounds, they were more at home with. They'd descended on Z's barely-conscious body with all the gravity the situation deserved and promised us several times that he was in good hands. We'd followed them here in a taxi . . . and then sat here for several hours, waiting to hear any scrap of news we could, too lost within our own thoughts to say much of anything to each other. I'd barely even thought about the seven million dollars that we no longer had. Nobody'd told us where Z'd been taken, but the hospital directory suggested he was somewhere in the Jorgensen Wing . . . which did *not* improve my mood.

I'd spent the first couple hours glued to my smartphone, looking up articles on stomach wounds, and feeling worse and worse as the consensus built—serious injuries were all but unsurvivable. I should've blackened the screen after the third article, but I kept reading, desperate to find one that disproved the others. There *were* none, though—just more corroborating evidence.

Every ten minutes or so, I'd taken a break to check the news-o-sphere for anything about Kira. Twitter mentioned a minor turf war in Weehawken, but not the car chase that'd been going on just blocks away. A couple of sites had short articles already up, but they'd been even less informative than I'd expected. There hadn't been anything concrete about the operation in the Catskills, either—just mentions that the site'd seen increased levels of police activity that afternoon. Each time I failed to find new information, I went back to reading medical articles and looking at pictures of open wounds.

Eventually, I'd seen enough and shoved the phone away. But then there was nothing to occupy my mind, keep it insulated from the ever-creeping shadows darkening its surface. The magazines on the tables were vapid and uninteresting, filled with pictures of smiling models with glowing skin and perfect teeth, and their bright colors kept invading my vision no matter where I turned.

Kira. They all reminded me of Kira. She never would've become a model, but she easily *could've*— she'd looked the part, besides her scar. Finally, I ended up turning all the magazines over so I didn't have to look at the covers anymore. It was almost a relief when a nurse entered and made a beeline for us, despite my rising dread in anticipation of her words. She wasn't quite tall enough to look me in the eye, but she made an honest effort.

"You're here with Sam Pearson, right?" she asked with a tight smile, and when we looked at each other and hesitated, she nodded encouragingly—she could tell from our faces.

It'd felt *wrong* giving Z an alias that didn't start with, well, Z, but Lorenzo'd seemed aware of Z's many names, and any patient with a Z in his name would probably attract undue attention from anyone examining the hospital records. Addie and I had agreed that S was enough like Z to preserve the spirit of the naming schema while remaining subtle.

"I'm Nurse Morris," she said. "First things first, your friend's expected to make a full recovery—"

A large, relieved smile spread over my face, and Addie's brow unfurrowed slightly.

"—within a couple weeks. He's a very lucky young man. The bullet missed the abdominal cavity and passed through the muscle on the way out."

I'd done enough scattered research in the past few hours to understand what good news this was.

"Please," said Addie with a quaver developed over long hours of practice. "We'd like to see him."

Nurse Morris's face scrunched in sympathy. "He's still in surgery. You can see him when he wakes up, but he's lost a lot of blood and mustn't be excited."

Addie opened her eyes wider, but Nurse Morris was unmoved. "I *promise* you he's in no immediate danger, and I will let you know immediately if that changes, or when he's awake."

"We'll wait," I said.

It was five more hours before Z was lucid enough to talk—five hours of sterilized air, small plastic cups of water, and furtive looks out the window in case someone'd been sent after us to finish the job. By the time Nurse Morris gave us the green light, the night outside was already dissolving into a cold blue.

Down long gleaming aisles she led us (I shuddered involuntarily as we passed the Jorgensen Wing's threshold), up two floors in an elevator so shamefully musty I could barely believe it was part of the same building, and finally to a door that looked like every other door on the hall. I memorized the room number—two twenty-three—just in case.

After a firm reminder from Nurse Morris that Z should under *no circumstances* be excited, we were allowed entrance.

"Hey," croaked Z as we stepped into the room.

He was propped up in the hospital equivalent of a reclining chair, bandages wrapped tightly around his torso. Strapped to his arm was a strange device that beeped steadily. There was an IV in his other arm, presumably so food didn't have to interact with his stomach, and seeing it made my own stomach rumble as it remembered how long it'd been since I'd eaten.

I was hungry enough to consider *hospital food.* Imagine that.

Z's eyes locked on me, then slowly moved across to Addie. He frowned. "Kira?"

Not trusting myself to speak, I shook my head.

Shock, pure naked shock, imploded across Z's face.

"I'm so sorry," whispered Addie.

Z's mouth worked as he tried to get himself under control—and failed. He let out a strangled groan that, coming from someone with more energy, might've been a yell, and then fell silent. Addie slipped from my side and laid a hand on one of his shoulders, which shook with quiet tears. Nurturing, comforting. It was what Z needed— but we couldn't afford it.

"Z," I said. "We don't have time right now."

Their eyes snapped back on me. Addie was looking disdainful, like she couldn't believe how stupid I was being. But Z . . .

His eyes were flashing with unsuppressed hatred, mouth a narrowed, furious slit. I got the sense that if he were feeling stronger, he'd rise and attempt to choke the life out of me.

But someone had to be the bad guy, and as leader, that was my responsibility.

"We're exposed here," I said. "The people who attacked us could find us at any second, and the hospital won't dissuade them. We gotta hide somewhere." Addie was brimming with undisguised contempt at this point, but I pressed on. "And not at home—they'll be watching those, and at this point, they'll stop at nothing to take us out. Lorenzo takes attacks on him *very* personally."

"What part of *don't excite him* don't you—" Addie began, but Z cut her off.

"I ain't going nowhere. I've got a fucking IV in my arm and I'd like to see y'all smuggle me out."

"It's dangerous—"

"They ain't giving me a choice. Now that's settled, I'd like some *time* to mourn my *friend.*"

Somehow, Z's voice, weak and almost monotone, was able to communicate just what he thought of me right then.

"Alright then. Mourn. But just know we're on the clock."

Z didn't deign to respond. He took deep breath after deep breath, and Addie clamped down harder on his shoulder while still glaring daggers at me.

Z looked up at her. "How'd she . . . "

"Heroic sacrifice," said Addie grimly. "Probably with a smile on her face."

"To save *you* bastards."

"You don't sound happy," I noted.

"You fucking *think?*"

Silence, as the arm-machine beeped away.

"Addie, help me here. We gotta figure out what we're doing."

"Give him some time," said Addie. She was looking past me, face even more shadowed than usual in the poorly-lit room.

"Listen to your girlfriend," said Z. "*Some* of us actually cared about Kira and need time to—"

"We've *had* time," I hissed. "Hours of it, in that waiting room while you were out cold. Don't you *dare* pretend to care more than we do. But the thing is, we need to keep our families safe *and* a place to stay."

"Not my problem. You figure it out," snapped Z with a force that left him coughing weakly, and wincing at every cough.

We waited politely for the coughs to subside, and in that time, Z's expression softened.

"Okay," he relented. "I've got an uncle in Manhattan with some spare rooms. He'll do me a favor. I'll call him and explain. Then I'll join you when they let me out."

"But if they come back—"

"—I'll worry about it then."

Beep. Beep. Beep.

"Okay," I said. "Sounds good. Make sure to tell him we aren't staying long."

I just needed enough time to get us ready to leave the state, maybe the country. Before we were attacked again. Before three became two.

"This is just because she would've wanted me

to," said Z, closing his eyes. "I'm putting my family in danger for you *again*, Jace. Don't you fucking make any *mistakes*."

"Again," I said. "We'll only need to be there a few days." A few days to pack, plan, figure out what to tell our families. And then we'd be gone.

I didn't know if Lorenzo'd be satisfied with us just fleeing. We'd have to spend the rest of our lives looking over our shoulders. But starting a new life in Europe certainly increased the time and effort it'd take him to pursue revenge. Maybe it'd take him so long he'd forget why he was angry.

And maybe pigs would fly.

SIX

Z'S UNCLE WAS TALL AND BROAD CHESTED, BUT with a relatively small head that made him look like the result of an unfortunate body-splicing accident. It was topped with graying hair and furnished with a small, also-graying goatee. The first thing he made clear was that he would *not* tolerate any bullshit.

"Zarius says you're in some trouble," he'd said in a voice that more matched his body than his head. "He's a good kid, and I'm happy to do his friends a favor. But," and here, his voice'd dropped a half-octave and I'd felt the full force of his glare, making me sink a few inches into the Earth, "I have no intention of getting caught in it. You keep your heads down while you're here, stay out of trouble. We've seen enough tragedy this year. I suspect either of you's been drawing any gang-related activity to my house, and you'll be staying just long enough to pack. You understand?"

We had.

"Good. And no . . . well, no *teenage* business."

A few awkward clarifications later, we'd determined he was referring to sex, drugs, booze, loud music . . . , all those classic scourges of the aging. Somewhat reluctantly, Addie and I had agreed to keep our clothes on.

But then, we'd also promised to stay out of trouble. We hadn't meant *that* promise, and if you were already gonna break *one* . . . Well, I'd broach the possibility with her when she got back tonight. I'd sent her out through the city—disguised, of course—to get wind of the Mafia's recent activities. Information was an important component of any campaign, and one I was sorely lacking.

Mr. Douglas—the uncle—was at work until six, so I had the house to myself. I'd made myself an omelette for lunch, and it wasn't bad if you slathered it in ketchup and pretended hard enough. I was spitting out some eggshell I'd accidentally bitten down on when my phone vibrated.

sup mothafucka

It was from Kira.

I sat there, paralyzed with shock, for maybe a year. By the time my fingers were working again, she'd sent a follow-up.

where you at?

There was no way in hell she'd survived. But if anyone *could've*, it'd be Kira. And the texts definitely *sounded* like her.

I *wanted* to believe it. I wanted to believe *anything* that pointed towards Kira's still being alive. But belief had consequences—consequences I couldn't afford. So I fought back the rising tide of hope and forced myself to think *rationally*.

Which was more likely? That Kira'd escaped

death at the hands of her pursuers, or that she . . . Well, hadn't? The second, surely.

Then who, if not Kira? But that was easy—the Mafia, having recovered her phone, now trying to find us. That was consistent with "Kira" asking where I was. But wouldn't the real Kira ask the same thing?

The message's composition meant nothing either way—anyone could've looked back through her text history to get a feel for her style.

To buy time, I sent the text Jason'd send if he *weren't* considering all this, which was, holy shit.

To which "Kira" responded yea im p cool. told u id be fine

My finger hovered over the keyboard, coming down most of the way and then drawing back a few times . . . and then I hit "call".

The person on the other end picked up immediately. "Yo, boss. Everything okay?"

It was *unmistakably* Kira's voice.

I staggered with relief and almost dropped the

phone. She wasn't dead. I hadn't failed her. All four of us could still make it together.

"You know how to talk?"

Right, I was on the phone. "Kira, you're *alive*," I said, relishing the feeling of the words as I said them.

"No, duh? You think I was dead?" Kira's laugh came loud and clear through the phone, and that was the final piece of proof I needed, if I hadn't been convinced from the moment she'd answered.

"Motherfuckers couldn't even touch me. Bomb-ass chase though. Lost them in Greenville. There was—"

But I'd taken the phone away from my ear at that point to text Addie and Z the news. Kira was still going when I lifted it again. "—Did a wicked drift onto the overpass, but of course they were coming to cut me off from Inverness, so I went into reverse . . . "

"Kira," I said loudly. My phone was already buzzing with responses. "I gotta go, but you can tell me everything in person. I'll text you where we are. You didn't go home, right?"

"You think I'm fucking stupid?"

Sometimes. "Just making sure. Glad you're okay. See you soon."

"Save the tears for my funeral. Kira out."

I stood there for a while just staring at the phone in my hand, before letting out a loud whoop of joy that I would've felt too self-conscious to indulge in if anyone'd been around. My phone was blinking, though, and I couldn't leave my friends hanging after dropping *that* bombshell. I answered question after question. No, this wasn't a joke. No, she didn't mention she was injured. Yes, she'd known to stay away from her house. Yes, she was headed to Mr. Douglas's. And finally (to Addie), yes, you can put the mission on hold and come see her.

I heard the door open about a half-hour later. Doorbells (or even knocks) had never been Kira's style. She just busted right in. Footsteps came from the hallway and before I could consider the possibility that they belonged to someone hostile, Kira strode proudly into the room. She looked downright *exhausted,* and was still bruised and bandaged from her fight with Troglodyte, but she was definitely, without a doubt, *alive.* All decorum abandoned, I ran over and hugged her as tightly as I could . . . until her breathing hitched and I remembered she was still recovering.

"Glad you're okay too, squirt," said Kira. I could feel myself grinning like an idiot at the sound of her voice. "Nice pad. Got any food?"

I indicated my omelette. Kira stared at it, probably trying to decide if it qualified as edible.

"I'll check the fridge," she said, and turned away from me, leaving hundreds of questions to burn unasked in my mouth. She settled on smearing cream cheese on some ham and rolling it, taquito-like, into a cylinder.

While she ate, I tried unsuccessfully to put my curiosity out of my head and turned back to my notebook, where I'd been hard at work planning our next moves. Not having money was making that harder than it should've been.

"Yo, Kira. You didn't happen to get away with the cash, did you?"

Kira swallowed a mouthful of ham. "Sorry, boss. Wasn't an option."

I'd kinda figured, but I couldn't help but feel disappointed. "It's cool."

Once Kira'd licked her fingers clean, she ambled over to my chair and looked down at my scribbles. The page was full of hastily-penned inferences, statistics, and schematics, a point-by-point list of goals . . . and some crudely drawn pictures I was doing my best to write around.

Kira squinted at them. "Who's been drawing dicks?"

"That was you. You drew them all over this notebook."

"Oh, right." Kira chuckled. She looked at her creations with an appraising eye. "These are pretty good."

I rolled my eyes.

"Huh," said Kira, peering at my list of possible countries to flee to. "Copenhagen hasn't closed its borders yet, you know."

Copenhagen. My pen hovered over the page as I weighed the merits and disadvantages . . . and then I realized, to my surprise, that Kira'd just tacitly endorsed fleeing to another country. "You aren't gonna argue with me about leaving? I figured I'd have to fight you tooth and nail."

"I dunno." Kira cracked her knuckles. "Yesterday, that would've been true. I guess what with the car chase and all, it makes sense we can't stay. Puts things into perspective."

That was maybe the most mature thing I'd ever heard Kira say.

"What?" she said, seeing my expression. "Part of winning's knowing what fights're unwinnable. If I gotta leave my family forever either way, might as well be the way where I'm still alive. Z's the same, he'll understand even if he hates it. Especially since he actually *was* shot."

"I . . . I'm glad you understand." I still wasn't sure what alternate-universe Kira'd replaced the one I was used to, who'd have charged into Little Italy on horseback looking for trouble, but I wasn't complaining. I shoved aside my notebook. "Now tell me what happened after we got out before I explode from curiosity."

"Might as well wait for Addie," said Kira coyly. "I don't wanna tell it twice."

Despite my every effort to loosen her tongue, her mouth remained stubbornly closed. I was almost screaming with frustration by the time Addie returned, which was thankfully not much later. Like me, she immediately swept Kira into a giant hug, which had Kira blinking uncomfortably and awkwardly patting her on the back. "I don't get it. You kids were *worried*?"

"You," Addie declared, "are an absolute *idiot*, Kira Applewood, and we love you for it."

Kira didn't look the least bit offended.

We sat down in the living room and swapped stories, making sure to keep Z—who would've walked out of the hospital right then if they'd let him—caught up. Kira's tale was as thrilling as it was almost certainly exaggerated. According to her, she'd ramped off a pickup truck, leaped from her driver's seat into another car's open window and wrested control over the wheel from its own driver, and sword-fought a dozen mobsters on an overpass by the light of the full moon (which'd been a sliver in the sky that night).

It was by far the fakest story I'd ever heard. But none of it was more impossible than Kira's survival itself, and *that* was obviously true . . . so why quibble the details? We were smiling, laughing, riding the sheer *joy* of Kira's continued existence. She could've said she'd hidden in the lost city of Atlantis and we'd have accepted it without question.

Next was Addie's turn. She'd scrapped her mission early to see Kira's triumphant return in person, but it sounded like she'd gotten all the information we needed in the short time she'd been out.

"Turns out the stereotype about the Mafia conducting all their business in person is true, or I'd have been done *much* faster," she said. "Luckily, they *do* keep written records of their meetings . . . and *valchiria* can go pretty much anywhere without being questioned. It wasn't even enciphered—well, it was mostly in Italian, but that's no problem for *me*."

That last bit was delivered with as much smugness as she could pack into seven syllables.

What she'd discovered was equal parts grim and unsurprising. Lorenzo Michaelis'd indeed escaped both Derek's teams *and* the net of officers. There was still a mountain-wide manhunt in full swing, and more and more Bonanno "soldiers" (most of which'd been deployed at that location) were being confirmed captured every hour. A few who'd fought back were dead.

Lorenzo was not, as you might imagine, pleased with any of this.

It was Genovese hit men who'd ambushed our car that night, the result of a hasty Bonanno-Genovese alliance. Both families were combing the city for us, following leads, shadowing known associates, and—as expected—watching our houses. Lorenzo was trying to bring the other families on board, and while Addie hadn't explicitly confirmed this last bit, she could infer it as easily as I—he was using the alliance to push for the title of *Capo Di Tutti Capi*—Boss of All Bosses.

Addie didn't know what he'd *do* with that power once he had it, but I could guess it'd be bad news for us.

"Luckily," I pointed out, "it's not our problem. We're leaving, remember?"

Addie shifted uncomfortably. "Yeah, about that . . . we won't be safer."

"What do you mean?"

The answer, when it came, should've been obvious—there was a price on our collective heads, advertised internationally. Lorenzo wasn't willing to entrust the task of our murder to the Mafia alone.

Two million each, alive or dead. Ten million for the whole team. Under other circumstances, I would've been flattered (Lucas too, would've been proud of me for finally being worth something). As it was, all I could think about was the quality of professional killer such a sum would attract.

Kira shook her head. "This asshole really hates us. What'd we ever do to him?"

"You mean . . . besides target his organization, indirectly incite a crackdown on organized crime, and try to catch him in a police ambush . . . twice?"

Addie winced. "Yeah, he's not going to let that go."

Ten million dollars. I'd *pay* that much to take the bounty off the market. But Lorenzo'd never agree to that—it was personal now. Even if he did, how could I even gather that much cash in the first place? Even the fortune we'd had to leave in the Civic's trunk wouldn't have paid it in full, and I didn't even have *that* anymore. How to *get* ten million dollars?

Well, besides the . . . *obvious* . . .

Or, now that I was thinking it . . . why *not* the obvious?

"I was never gonna let us leave without some cash to start our new lives," I said with a smile. "Ten million sounds about right."

"You want to turn ourselves in and claim the bounty?" said Addie. "Someone actually tried that once, you know. Didn't go so well for him. They just laughed and tossed him in jail."

"Yeah, that'd be stupid," I said. "No, I'm suggesting we die for a bit."

"Fake our deaths," said Addie slowly. "Have someone step up to claim the bounty, then pass it along to us, probably for a nominal fee . . . it could work. But the mob will want proof, probably bodies—"

"—So we'd need bodies. Z's probably best buds with someone at a morgue, I'll ask him right now—"

"—We'll need to disfigure the bodies so nobody can tell it's not us, like in a fire or—"

"—Gas explosion," we said simultaneously, and then high fived.

Kira perked up at that—she'd been sulking in her chair, as she usually did during planning meetings. She liked to be able to follow conversations, and had never quite gotten over the fact that when ideas were flying thick and fast, she couldn't keep up.

Still, even while sulking, she was in a better mood than I'd seen her in *months*. I wondered if the high-adrenaline chase'd gotten something out of her system, but that seemed too good to be true. I resolved to watch her closely in case she showed signs of relapsing.

"Big surprise," I said, looking up from my phone. "Z's old dealer works in a morgue now.

Z thinks he can get us in, but he's also really con-fused about why we suddenly need dead bodies. Should I tell him?"

"Nah," said Kira, smirking. "Let him wonder."

SEVEN

"**P**APERWORK," I SAID.

Addie dutifully held up the hotel contract we'd signed. "Check."

"Room key."

That was Addie again. "Check."

"Plastic explosives."

Kira smiled toothily, somehow managing not to erupt in full-blown maniacal laughter. "Check."

"Corpses."

"Check," said Z morosely. He'd drawn the short straw—as we'd all known he would—and been assigned responsibility for our formaldehyde-filled surrogates.

Getting them'd been a whole lot easier than I'd prepared for. When Z'd intimated he knew someone at the morgue, I expected we'd have to abuse his trust and carefully smuggle out four bodies.

Instead, Z—who'd been released from the hospital after another week of care—had walked right up to the guy, and after a brief discussion, gotten him to look the other way as we examined the bodies, loaded them onto gurneys, and dumped them unceremoniously into the back of a truck Kira'd "borrowed" earlier that morning. He'd been rather amiable about it, really—taken our money, warned us to look out for other employees, and turned back to his newspaper, whistling softly.

I dunno what I'd expected from a morgue worker, but *that* wasn't it.

And so we'd set about the task of finding four recently dead, currently unclaimed corpses that resembled us enough that they could, if subjected to heavy enough burns, pass as our own. I was trying *really* hard not to think of the families who might miss these bodies later, but at the end of the day, they'd survive without them . . . which is more than could be said for us.

Finding four dead teenagers on a randomly selected New York morning wasn't a walk in the park, but I was actually thankful for that. We finally managed to find one small enough to pass as Addie, but "my" corpse was listed as age twenty-seven, and Kira's was twenty-five. She had black hair and a stomach tattoo, but I figured the hair'd burn off, and it's not like anyone could say Kira *hadn't* gotten a secret stomach tattoo at some point.

We'd vetoed Z's first find since it had an array of stab wounds across the chest, and an autopsy'd pick those up unless we ramped the "fire damage" aspect of our plan way up. Z was forced to settle for a sixteen-year-old victim of head trauma who was two inches shorter than him. This was a significant amount—and it was particularly important to get Z's body as accurate as possible given the number of people who'd probably attend his funeral—but hopefully nobody'd pull out a ruler and *measure* him.

It was kinda funny picturing all Z's friends meeting for his funeral and arguing about what his name'd been. But I didn't mention this—death was a touchy subject right now.

My own doppelgänger was nowhere near as handsome as me, of course, but a suitable match in other respects down to eye color. The retinas'd be destroyed in the conflagration either way, but the match made it feel a little more like destiny and a little less like grave-robbing.

"Sorry, pal," I'd said, patting the clammy body's forehead, "but you just might save my life."

Now he and our three other cadavers were piled on one of the local Biltmore's luggage trolleys, safely hidden beneath a draped sheet, and surrounded with the strongest air fresheners money could buy. They weren't helping much. But we'd anticipated the problems transporting corpses might create, and negotiated a room at the front desk *before* bringing them on-site. We just needed to wheel the trolley across the lobby to the elevator and we'd be practically home free.

"Too bad we won't be getting our deposit back," I mused. "Like, I can afford it, but *still*."

"You mean because coming back from the dead to claim it would be suspicious?" said Addie.

"Also, we're blowing up the room."

"Right. That too."

Once we'd blown up the bodies, David, a second cousin of Z's (who would, under no circumstances, make that connection known) would go to the Mafia and take credit for the deed. To that end, we'd checked into the hotel using our real names, just to make it plausible for him to've found us—and to "guarantee" that it was us who'd died. Addie had the documentation in hand to give David later, in case he needed to show it.

We'd also told him who to say sold him the explosives—Mike Lolan, with whom Z'd been able to strike an incredible deal. Lolan was hardly trustworthy, but he knew the value of customer service, and never disclosed information about his clientele to third parties. The Mafia'd have no way to falsify David's story—and why would they suspect? Mike Lolan sold to everyone.

None of us had any experience detonating plastic explosives, but that hadn't stopped Kira, who'd taken to it like a six-year-old to fruity candy. Nobody'd handed it to her, but she'd gotten her hands on it *anyway*, somehow, and hadn't let go since. None of us were dumb enough to trust her with it, but we were all too smart to try and take it from her. Plus, Kira hadn't quite exhausted the near-limitless amount of goodwill she'd generated simply by still being alive.

Knowing her, it'd be gone by sundown.

We were sitting ducks with a foul-smelling trolley, so waiting held no advantage. I gave Addie the signal.

Addie's task was to engage any employees in the lobby who looked like their job was to help newcomers—just a bit of conversation to distract them, make them less inclined to ask if we needed a hand with our cart. As she passed through the automatic doors, Kira hefted her backpack and slid the straps over her shoulders. I eyed it with some amount of trepidation.

But there was no confiscating it now, so I just followed Addie without comment. I had my own important part to play—well, really just getting to the elevators ahead of the corpse-trolley and making sure an empty one awaited it. The alternative was standing awkwardly in a hotel atrium (and/or a small, enclosed elevator with a bunch of strangers) while smuggling dead people, and while that hadn't even been *on* my list of things to never do before yesterday, it'd recently made the top ten.

The atrium was turquoise-tiled, brown-rugged, and well-lit. I felt like I was under a spotlight even though nobody was looking at me. Addie was engaging a concierge near the edge of my vision. I walked quickly by, deliberately not looking at anyone who looked like hotel staff.

It turned out an empty elevator was already waiting on the bottom floor. I held it open with one arm and waited while Kira and Z made their way across the floor, trolley in tow. They gave the lounge area a suspiciously wide berth, but made it to the elevator without incident, with Addie close behind. They passed me without a glance, like we were strangers.

"Sixty-fifth floor," Addie said to Kira. Kira hit the button and the "door close" button at the same time, and held them down until the elevator'd started moving, just like Tony and Cloudface'd done in Vegas. I wasn't sure if this particular elevator had that backdoor command to bypass other floors programmed in, but either it did or we just got lucky, because we reached our floor without anyone joining us for the ride and asking why our luggage smelled like vanilla and corpse. All of us except Kira were breathing through our shirts by the time the doors opened.

It was a refreshingly short journey from there to our room. Addie scouted ahead from corner to corner, making sure the hallways were clear—which they were. This entire level was mostly deserted, or so Kira'd said.

We reached our room without encountering anyone. Addie buzzed the door open and I held it while Z wheeled in his morbid cargo and stripped away the sheet.

Too bad we'd have to blow this room up, because it was *really* nice. Couldn't say much for the view, but that was a problem endemic to New York City, and nothing the Biltmore could be expected to fix. The rug was better quality than it needed to be, and *some* effort'd been made to match the colors with each other. You couldn't ask much more from a Biltmore room, and you *certainly* didn't have to aggressively remodel it with explosives.

But we'd already taken the minimal courtesy

of choosing a room near the top of the building, in a corner—and we'd done the best we could to choose one nobody was staying near. We'd staked the rooms out personally, and Kira'd taken a quick look in the system—if everything was accurate *and* nobody'd moved into those rooms in the past twenty-four hours (and why would they choose a room this high up given the space available below? This wasn't peak hotel season, so rooms were readily available), nobody'd be hurt.

Not that it would matter if they were, said Lucas chidingly. *It's you or them. The right answer in that scenario is always you.*

Sometimes I wonder if Lucas is completely unaware of game theory, or if he's an expert—and considered it a "How to Be a Bigger Asshole" guide.

"Holy tittyfucking yes," Kira was saying as she moved around the apartment. "It's what I always wanted. A nice room that's all my own, that I get to blow to fucking hell."

As she spoke, she was shaping charges, regarding

them with the eye of an artist, arranging furniture around them like macabre sculptures.

"How'd you get so good with those?" asked Z as he lifted his other self into the bed and tucked him under the covers.

"Natural talent, I guess."

Addie sat her own corpse in a chair by the table. Then, with just a hint of hesitation, she placed her computer, open, in front of it. We'd all backed up our data already, but I understood her reluctance. Computers were our *friends*.

It wasn't just them we were leaving here, to sell the illusion. IDs, debit cards, Starbucks gift cards . . . our wallets, basically. Our phones (or, old phones we'd bought for the purpose of blowing up). Anything you'd expect a teenager to have with him in a hotel.

Everything was fair game to be blown up. It was all replaceable. Our lives weren't.

I leaned my guy against the dresser. I had to stick one of his arms through a drawer handle, but he stayed up. It was probably better to have at least one guy standing, just in case the forensics team could tell if people were standing or sitting when the bombs went off. The skin was cold and leathery. I was gonna take the *longest* shower after this. And probably have nightmares.

Kira drew a bath for hers, rigged a couple detonators around the bathroom, then shut the door. The scene was set. We surveyed the tableau—some of us more proudly than others.

"This is disgusting," said Z.

"No kidding," said Kira, wrinkling her nose. But that's not how he'd meant it.

Creepy as the bodies were, I couldn't bring myself to leave. I can't explain why, exactly, but everyone else was wavering to and fro as well, so it wasn't just me.

"So, do we leave now, or . . . "

Addie shrugged. "I guess."

So we did. What more was there to do? Delays

were meaningless, regardless of the sentiment behind them.

We couldn't exit through the lobby (what if someone remembered seeing us exit safely just before our room exploded?), so we punched in the second floor and rode the elevator Earthward. Each new floor we reached, Kira's excited vibrating grew more and more intense, until she was practically giddy with glee.

The doors slid open on a thankfully deserted hotel corridor. After a quick search, we found the stairs and crouched in the alcove between the first and second floors. Here, we could rest easy knowing we wouldn't be interrupted—who'd take the stairs when there were elevators?

Unless, of course, the elevators weren't working. In case of fire, for example. But how likely was *that*?

In this particular instance, really fucking likely.

"Well, team," I said. "Ready to die?"

There were solemn nods from everyone except Kira, who flashed a jubilant thumbs up.

"Then detonate away."

Kira plunged a hand into her backpack.

High above me and to the east, I heard a loud *whump*. Then another, and another.

Alarms kicked in, two or three different ones, like the hotel's alarm system couldn't decide what'd just happened. There was a transcendent look on Kira's face, like she'd just learned Christmas lasted all of December.

"I suppose we're dead now," said Addie softly.

There was a pain on her face I couldn't place—and on Z's too, I realized. But a stampede of feet was approaching the staircase as people realized the elevators were offline, and there was no time to ponder what it could mean.

The people in the lobby now had more pressing things on their minds than a gaggle of teens among a stampede of evacuees, so I judged it safe to leave. We were among the first in the swell of the crowd through those automatic doors.

We left our whole lives behind us.

EIGHT

"YOU KNOW WHAT THEY DON'T TELL YOU ABOUT being dead?" Kira joked. "How much it feels like being alive."

We were seated around Mr. Douglas's living room, preparing our next move. Mr. Douglas himself would be at work for another few hours, and we'd be gone before he returned. Leaving everything we'd brought with us here, of course—because if we were dead, who'd have retrieved it?

Z frowned. "But who could say what being dead's like, except us?"

"Other dead people who're still alive," Kira retorted. "You know what I mean. Like Elvis."

Addie and I looked at each other, both trying to figure out whether she was kidding, or legitimately believed Elvis was still alive.

"But those people would have an interest in keeping their continued existence secret," said Addie. "So why tell anyone? Like, say Elvis walked up to you and started telling you what being dead was like?"

"I . . . I don't think I'd believe he's dead anymore."

"Exactly."

Kira's face screwed up in concentration as she tried to puzzle out the meaning of *that*, and I turned back to the television, sensing that the conversation'd ended for now. We'd been flipping between channels, staying with coverage of the hotel bomb. They'd gotten their hands on the hotel records about a half-hour ago, at which point they'd flashed them onto the screen, superimposed over whatever pictures they could grab off Facebook. *Kira Applewood. Jason Jorgensen. Zorro Davis.*

Addison Bristol. They didn't show the corpses—but they must've passed whatever test the twenty-four-hour news cycle'd deemed appropriate. Meaning, I'd be surprised if they examined them for more than ten seconds.

Our cellphones were already off, or the calls would've started rolling in from parents and friends desperate to check in just in case the news'd messed up somehow. It'd be a while before I'd consider it safe to turn them on again.

Currently, the newscaster was earnestly discussing the possibility that there'd been foul play involved, given the explosion's highly localized nature.

"—Say the damage to other rooms was limited, as if the blast was shaped by a professional—"

Kira made no effort to hide her pride.

"Professional nuisance, more like," I said just loud enough that she could hear. She threw a pillow at my head.

"Not allowed!" said Addie sharply, catching it in

midair and returning it to its place on the couch. "We can't leave any signs someone was here after we died."

Kira rolled her eyes. "I still think y'all are too paranoid. Nobody actually pays attention to random strangers on the street—"

"I do," said Addie.

"—So there's no point to all this sneaking around and hiding. We've got a few hours left in the place we grew up, and we're gonna spend it in some stranger's house?"

"How would you *like* to spend it?" I asked.

"Saying bye to my family," she said immediately.

I laughed, but Kira wasn't so much as smiling.

"*Some* of us actually give a shit about our families," she said. "*Some* of us aren't exactly happy to be doing this. *Some* of us might've thought things through for another couple minutes before deciding sure, faking our deaths was the best plan. Y'know, if *we* were the ones who came up with the plans, instead of the ones who just followed along.

Like, did you think about what you were asking us to do? Really *think* about it?"

I looked at Addie and Z for backup, hoping they'd help me explain that I couldn't take anyone's feelings into account when constructing the plan with the greatest odds of success. Anything less and our chances of *actually* dying would shoot up unacceptably. But there was no sympathy in their faces—just reluctant agreement.

"Guys—"

"Listen to her," said Z. "What've *you* really sacrificed? You get to run far away from your dick of a dad and start over again, free. Like you always wanted. But the rest of us ain't like that. We got family here, and friends. And we're leaving all that behind because you say we gotta. Maybe you're right, but recognize it sucks for us."

"You can't—"

"You think about my mom at all? Not too long ago she lost her husband. Now you want her to bury her kid too. Is it *right* not to let her know I'm still okay?"

Everyone was focused on me, waiting . . . for some kind of penitence, I guess. Kinda ungrateful, if you ask me, but you can't always expect the appreciation you're due. And if it'd shut up the grumbling, I didn't mind giving them what they wanted.

"Fine," I said. "It's not right. It sucks. Whatever. Sorry." *For saving us all,* I silently added. I turned back towards the television, where the anchor was inviting people who knew us to call in.

Mid-sentence, he vanished as the TV screen darkened, powered off. Addie was holding the remote, and looking at me fiercely. Not angry-fierce, but fierce like she had something she was willing to fight for.

"We want to say goodbye."

In unison, almost creepily so, Kira and Z folded their arms in agreement.

I fought the sudden rush of irritation. "The

more people know we're alive, the shakier the plan gets. I thought you'd understand that, Addie. Maybe not these two, but you for sure."

She held my gaze without a trace of embarrassment. Not that there would've been one no matter *what* she felt.

"*These two*," snorted Z.

"You really wanna risk everything?" I said to Addie, ignoring Z for now. "If something goes wrong, if word gets out . . . "

"We'll make sure they understand why it needs to be a secret," said Addie. "Even if they let something slip, we'll be far away by then. The mob won't have the trail."

I rounded on Kira next. "You're gonna tell your parents why they need to pretend you're dead? After all you did to hide this part of your life from them?"

She shrugged. "I gotta do what I gotta do. But I'm not just leaving them."

It was at that moment that the doorbell rang . . . and the whole room froze.

You could really see how jumpy we were, despite our posturing. We could tell ourselves our precautions were keeping us safe, but did we really believe that if a doorbell was enough to put us into fight-or-flight mode?

No. We didn't. I was *expecting* the door, and *still* thought through several dozen ways things could've gone wrong. The mob could've discovered Mr. Douglas's family connection to Z, or traced the truck theft back to us, or heard about the missing bodies at the morgue, or—

My phone—my *other* phone, the one only four people had the number to—buzzed. Kira and Z jumped at the sudden sound.

It's me. Confirmation code 26: Chewbacca was killed by a moon.

"It's alright," I said casually, trying to pretend I hadn't frozen as badly as everyone else when the bell rang. Come in. Key's under the chair cushion, I texted back.

Nobody else was moving yet. "Who is it?" asked Addie hesitantly.

The front door opened with a slow creak, and I felt another, smaller, stab of fear. What if I'd misjudged? Derek was a professional, but he was a mercenary, and his services belonged to the highest bidder. If Lorenzo'd gotten to him . . .

But at the very least, he'd give us a chance to buy his loyalty back. Mercenaries who unexpectedly turn on their employers don't stay in business long. And if Derek weren't trustworthy in that sense, Lucas never would've put him on the list I'd used to find him—Lucas values loyalty highly.

"It's our money," I said, evading. There were footsteps in the hallway, and the others were squirming, thinking about running or hiding. But I stayed put, trying to look relaxed, and they all followed my lead in the end.

"Mr. Jorgensen," said Derek, stepping into

view. I'd always liked how he called me that, didn't infantilize me. It was a small gesture on his part, and I'm sure he knew the effect it had, but that didn't stop me from subconsciously preening a bit. "You're looking remarkably well, considering your reported condition."

He was holding a leather briefcase. I tried to not look at it, but knowing what was inside made that *very* difficult.

"Oh, you know how reliable the news is these days," I said. "I've never been better."

"What's *he* doing here?" said Kira.

Derek nodded towards her. "Ms. Applewood. Speaking of looking remarkably well . . . congratulations on your swift recovery. We were very worried. Are you—?"

"I was afraid the Mafia might be tailing David after paying him," I said, cutting off the sandy-haired mercenary. "I arranged with him and Derek to perform a covert handoff, so Derek could bring the money safely. You weren't followed?"

"If I was, I didn't notice," said Derek. He stepped forward and put the briefcase on the ground. "Nine-and-a-half million. You can count it."

"I trust you," I said. "A million of it's yours, if you give your word that as far as you're concerned, we died in that hotel."

Derek smiled ruefully. Then he knelt and snapped open the briefcase. "I can't believe you actually blew up a Biltmore. This job got way weirder than I expected."

"We didn't blow it up," I corrected. "The Mafia did."

"So they did," said Derek.

He didn't buy it, not for one second. But he knew the game he was expected to play. I was certainly making it worth his while.

He counted out ten stacks of money right there on the floor, all in crisp hundreds. Then he loaded it all into a paper bag Addie'd gotten him once it'd become clear he'd need it. He stood, holding the bag, and looked me right in the eye.

"I'm correct when I assume I'll never see you again, Mr. Jorgensen?"

"There's nobody to see," I replied. "He died in a hotel bombing earlier this morning. You may see someone who looks like him, years from now, but I wouldn't expect him to know your name."

A crisp, professional nod from Derek. "Understood."

"Due to his sudden departure, you may reasonably conclude he'll no longer be paying you. As such, your team's free to find a different employer—there's no expectation that you continue your current job."

Another nod. "Thank you, sir. Makes sense."

I swallowed. My next words felt awkward in my mouth, and I found myself questioning how appropriate they were as I said them. But they needed to be said.

"If he were alive today . . . he'd thank you, Derek. For a job well done. For your courage, and your loyalty. He couldn't have done it without you."

"You're quite welcome, Mr. Jorgensen," said Derek softly. You could almost see the ghost of a smile through his stubble. "It was a pleasure."

He nodded one last time to me, and then to the other three. And then he turned and walked back down the hallway. Again, the door creaked open, and shut in the wake of his departure.

Kira was half right, in that nobody'd told me how being dead felt. It felt—appropriately, I guess—like my life was ending, bit by bit. It felt like shit.

I felt a tingling on my back and turned around to see Kira glaring at me like she was sighting down a sniper rifle. "So *he* can know, but our parents can't?"

It was different. So *obviously* different I couldn't even find the words to explain it. You get it, I'm sure. I know Addie got it too, but at this point, she didn't care how intellectually honest Kira's arguments were. She was latching onto whatever she could.

"If the plan can survive Derek knowing, our families should be allowed to know too," she said.

She folded her arms across her chest. Beside her, Kira and Z moved into position, forming a united front. That's when I knew I was beaten. Even if I forbade them, they'd just ignore me.

My anger swirled inside me like brandy in a snifter. *Let* them jeopardize everything for their precious goodbyes. "Fine. You can see them."

"Jesus Christ, we don't need your *permission*," said Z darkly. I ignored him.

"And I guess you just *forgot* to tell us about Derek? Remember how you've got a problem with not telling us shit we need to know?

I ignored him again. It was getting to be a habit. He could try saying nicer things if he wanted people to talk to him.

"Just remember to make it *clear* our lives depend on staying dead in the eyes of the world," I warned. "Our flight leaves from LaGuardia at six forty-seven, so let's meet there two hours early.

That gives you a good five hours to do whatever you need."

I'd be lucky if they didn't somehow ruin everything the moment they left my sight. We were supposed to be *professionals*, and this was the most amateur move I could imagine—the kind of "What Not to Do" example you see in how-to guides. "*Do* straighten out the details of your new life immediately. *Don't* immediately tell someone you're actually alive."

But surely they could function without me for a few *hours*, right? We were all adults, after all.

"Addie, you pick up our new passports and IDs—Courtney's got them at her place in the Bronx. You can hand them out at the airport."

"Got it."

"Then grab your share of cash off the floor and let's get moving," I said. "See you guys at the airport."

It was a little more brusque than I'd intended,

but I was *pissed*. Why poke a perfectly good plan full of holes like that?

I wish I'd had some inkling of the future as I walked out into the crisp morning sunlight, backpack stuffed with bills. I would've made more of an effort to inject kindness into my voice. Would've said something meaningful. Or at least just paid more attention to my words so I wouldn't struggle to recall them later. But at the time, there was no reason to do any of those things.

I had no idea I was never gonna make it to the airport.

NINE

I HAD ONE LAST CRIME TO COMMIT BEFORE LEAVING the States, and it was the easiest of all possible crimes—stealing from myself.

There's always talk of the "perfect crime," but it's hard to find one more perfect than that. Nobody's gonna report it, nobody's gonna notice anything's missing, and the victim doesn't even lose out. Everyone wins.

Now you're thinking, "Well, nobody really gains anything either," and you have a point. But in this situation, it'd be suspicious if stuff vanished from my apartment *without* looking like it'd been stolen. The apartment wasn't in my name, just in case the Mafia ever came after me (Past Me fucking *called it*), but I expected the pieces'd come together once "Jeff Stamos" spent enough time missing to get people assigned to his case.

For the first time in my life, I opted to take the subway. Every ingrained habit screamed at me to hail a taxi instead, but taxis were risky now, as was any service that relied on face-to-face communication. A taxi driver could recognize my face from the news and ask awkward questions, or just tip off the authorities. Much of the subway system was automated at this point, and it was easy in the shadowed understations to go unnoticed by the streaming New York crowd, who were always desperate to be anywhere but where they were. I'd never be as good at it as Addie, but just hanging around her'd taught me some tricks. Stay close to the wall, but don't hug it. Make sure you're never in anyone's way. Look busy.

Just in case, Kira'd lent me one of her giant hoodies, which despite being a literal fashion disaster, sporting several inconsequential logos in prominent locations, and smelling faintly of sweat and stale beer, adequately covered my head from the back and sides—and my button-up shirt, which apparently was enough to put me in the top percentage of dressers among subway-goers by default.

I puzzled out the map system, fed some bills into the ticket machine, and descended further into the bowels of the Earth. I was trying to frame this as experiencing New York one last time, but it wasn't helping, especially not when my subway arrived and I saw the space I was expected to fit into. Bracing myself, I squeezed in, hoping nobody realized how much my backpack's contents were worth. Riots have broken out over less.

Needless to say, I stumbled out the automatic doors, heaving in huge gasps of dank underground air the moment it reached my station. Someone should've been waiting for me with a trophy or words of congratulations, but there was only a lone busker with a violin, staring at the uncaring traffic with resignation born of experience as he played.

I tossed a twenty into his case as I passed. Not usual behavior for me, but there was a familiarity in him that felt like looking into a mirror, despite the fact that our situations bore little resemblance to each other. Maybe it was as simple as two people trying to make the best out of a bad situation.

And besides, I could afford it. I could afford to do the same for every busker in New York City.

He saw the denomination as I dropped it in and looked up to thank me, but I was already gone, obscured by my hoodie. I hadn't done it so he could recognize my kindness—being recognized at all wasn't on my list of things to do.

The apartment building was just a block from the station, one of many skyscrapers contributing to the famous New York skyline. It hadn't been my home long, but I'd been getting attached. Now I was abandoning it.

Still, it was getting off easier than the *last* room I'd rented.

I retreated even deeper into my hoodie as I walked through the lobby, but I shouldn't have bothered—the attendant was buried in a newspaper and nobody else so much as looked my way. Ironically enough, they were distracted by footage of the bombed Biltmore playing on a television in the corner. Getting out again'd be more difficult—suitcases tended to attract attention—but I had some ideas on that subject. I hadn't decided what I'd be stealing yet, besides the cash and electronics. Maybe some clothing? Just about all my worldly possessions were easily replaceable across the pond, so it made sense to prioritize things with sentimental value.

Oh, and my financial records. Actually, just about everything in that cabinet. Wouldn't want investigators stumbling across the notebooks I kept filling with criminal enterprises. And everything in the "sentimental" file (shoved to the very back in case someone else opened the drawer) was irreplaceable, from a certain point of view.

As soon as I got through the door, the hoodie came off. Maybe Kira wouldn't notice if I just left it here—but unfortunately, leaving something of Kira's at the scene wasn't an option. Then I unslung and unzipped my backpack. Sure enough, the money was still there. Seed money for my new life in Europe. I ran my fingers through it appreciatively.

But I'd have time to celebrate my riches later, and right now I was on the clock. I dropped the backpack next to the hoodie and walked over to the vast pane of glass that made up my living room wall for one final look at the city.

It'd been a lovely view when I first moved in— now, one of the giant billboards displayed a garish *Jorgensen International* ad. As I gazed out at the streets below, Lucas's smirking mug stared back at me. He'd done it on purpose, of course—I guess just to remind me that even though I'd moved out,

I'd never fully escape him. At least there weren't any billboards high enough to cast a shadow over my apartment. The symbolism would've been just too much for me to stand.

If I put my annoyance at the billboard aside, though, I could lose myself appreciating the sheer scale of what humanity'd accomplished. We'd dragged ourselves out of the primordial ooze and built our way towards the heavens.

Everything the light touched was our kingdom, and New York was the city that never sleeps.

It moved beneath me, a machine with countless pieces all working in tandem. I saw people hurrying about on the sidewalks below, intent on business, each with their own story to tell. Cars shifted and stalled and honked. A police siren wailed in the distance. Business as usual.

I'd miss New York, but perhaps I could get used to somewhere quieter. A beach town, maybe, with a luxury bed-and-breakfast and a thriving gambling scene.

But time wouldn't stop while I stood and stared, and I needed to be at the airport in a few hours, so I took a mental snapshot and ripped my eyes away. I had errands besides this one to attend to. If I could wrap this up quickly, I might have time for a quick visit to Creedmoor.

Yeah, I was a total hypocrite since I'd resisted the idea of telling our parents we were alive, but it's not like anyone'd believe Mom even if she *did* tell. I'd need to work out a way in without giving my identity, but plans were no problem for *me*.

First things first, though.

I retrieved my suitcase from the storage closet and placed the contents of my file cabinet carefully within. The empty drawer remained on the ground, like I'd been hunting for important paperwork and couldn't be bothered to put the cabinet back together afterwards. Once I finished packing, I was really gonna let loose and *trash* the place, but there was no rule saying I couldn't start early.

Then the bedroom sweep. There wasn't much

in there, if I remembered correctly, but what little there was'd be important. Sure enough, one of Addie's necklaces was lying on the bedside table, chain pooled beneath an inset amethyst. I scooped it up. She hadn't complained about missing it, but I knew she'd appreciate having it back. What I hadn't bought her (or she hadn't stolen) had been in her family at least two generations. She'd wanna pass it down someday.

As I looked across the room for more potential knickknacks, I noticed something incongruous with my expectations—an envelope, perched on one of my pillows. I hadn't noticed it before because the paper blended in with the pillowcase.

I noticed that I was confused.

Had Addie left it? I tried to remember whether she would've had an opportunity. Had she been with me when I left the apartment last? But of course, it *was* Addie—she could've borrowed my key and slipped in any time over the past week during one of her excursions.

Or the Mafia'd somehow traced "Jeff Stamos" back to me, and the envelope'd explode in my face when I opened it, or transmit contact poison through my skin into my bloodstream and kill me.

Or Lucas wanted me to know he was still watching, or something more sinister.

Or—but I was being stupid. No need to theorize about who'd placed the letter when I could just open it and find out. It *probably* wasn't a letter bomb.

I lifted it gingerly. It was a normal weight, and I didn't feel any suspicious burning sensations on my hand, so it was probably fine to open—

And then came three distinct knuckle-raps on the door.

I froze. My mind tried to generate a hypothesis for who it might be and came up blank. Whoever it was would *probably* leave if I just stayed here and pretended nobody was home . . .

There was a sharp *click* I recognized as the sound of my front door unlocking, and my hopes plummeted. Someone was about to *enter* my apartment, and I had no idea who they were or why they were here.

I thought about hiding, or darting into the bathroom, or at least positioning myself behind the door with something heavy. I thought about all these things, but I was frozen. Inactive. It was all I could do to control my breathing.

The door swung open and didn't close. I heard steps in the living room. My veins got colder and colder as they approached the bedroom door . . .

A pregnant pause . . .

The door burst free of its frame and my world became noise and confusion.

"On your knees! Hands behind your head! Don't move!"

I stared dumbly at three officers of the law— one framed in the doorway, one in the room with his nightstick out, and the third peeking in from behind. They were still shouting, repeating commands, getting increasingly agitated, and I decided it'd probably help matters if I obeyed. So I got down onto the floor, dropped the envelope, and followed their instructions. The largest one—the one in the doorway—came forward and cuffed me roughly while the third spoke rapidly into a radio. I caught the word "apprehended" through a whirlwind of bewilderment.

"What's going on?" I heard my mouth say, and received no response from the officer, who, once he'd finished cuffing me, dragged me to the wall and sat me against it. He relieved me of my phones and wallet, patted my pockets to make sure they were empty, then looked up in my face and frowned suddenly.

"I know you from somewhere?"

He'd recognized me from the morning news.

Somehow, that brought me out of my confused daze as I realized *everything* was at stake right now. The Mafia had people inside the NYPD. If these cops realized I was the same Jason Jorgensen who'd died this morning, the news'd travel.

If I didn't make the rendezvous at LaGuardia, couldn't even tell the group something'd gone wrong . . . they might not leave without me. They'd think the Mafia didn't know they were alive, but they'd be in even more danger than before.

I *had* to escape. Or at least warn them somehow. "No," I said.

The first officer, the one with the nightstick, slid open the drawer of my bedside table. Whatever he saw made him nod grimly. I was still trying to remember what I'd stashed there when he pulled out a large bag filled with white powder. And I was willing to bet every penny I owned it wasn't flour.

"It's not mine," I said immediately, knowing how futile it sounded as I said it. The cop closest to me—whose nametag identified him as Larry—laughed out loud.

The bag was *enormous*. There were *Scarface* nose-skiing levels of cocaine in there—assuming it *was* cocaine, but if this was a setup to get me arrested, the perpetrator'd be dumb to not use the real stuff. A bag that size was worth a small fortune. Someone'd spent *that much money* to put me away.

Again, it would've been flattering if it weren't screwing me over so badly.

It was probably the same person who'd left the envelope—unless *two* people'd independently broken into my apartment in the past week, which didn't seem particularly likely. I regretted not just opening the damned thing when I'd had the chance.

But maybe—if I was incredibly lucky, and the person who'd set me up wasn't too bright—the letter'd vindicate me. Maybe my enemy'd felt an ill-advised need to gloat via letter, not realizing I could just *show the cops*. Probably not . . . but people've done dumber things. It was within the bounds of possibility.

"I know what this looks like," I tried. "But you gotta believe me. This whole thing's a setup. I've never seen that bag before."

"Sure, kid," said a cop. "Save it for court."

"That letter on the ground'll prove it," I said. I was desperate, and this was my only out.

The cop eyed it skeptically. "What's it say?"

"See for yourself."

"You don't gotta do that," said Larry. "Take it in as evidence and let's be outta here."

But the cop was already opening the envelope.

"That's tampering with evidence," Larry protested.

The paper made a crinkling sound as the cop drew it from the envelope and unfolded it. He barely even *glanced* at the letter before looking back at me.

"C'mon, you didn't even read it."

He looked at me like I was crazy, and my hopes withered and died. "Nice try, kid. Let's go."

So much for *that* plan. There was no way around it—I was gonna miss my flight. But it wasn't over yet. I had some time to work out an escape. I didn't have to make a full getaway—just get a message to the group letting them know the situation.

It'd be helpful, then, to know as much about the situation as possible.

"Alright," I said. "But first . . . Can *I* see that letter?"

The cops looked at each other helplessly. Finally, the one who'd opened it said, "Sure."

He held the piece of binder paper in front of my face so I could read it without being uncuffed. It was just one sentence long, plus a signature, but it took almost a full minute to read because my brain kept refusing to believe what my eyes insisted was there.

Now we're even
-Z

TEN

HE'D NEVER FORGIVEN ME.

It was so obvious now, I couldn't believe I hadn't seen it before—his oscillation between hostility and cordiality, his carefully aimed taunts, his undercurrent of resentment even when discussing nothing of consequence. All these months, he'd blamed me.

It didn't seem *enough*, somehow, to justify jeopardizing our escape. But then, I didn't know the thought process he'd gone through, and I'm sure it made perfect sense to *him*. This was hardly a spur-of-the-moment plan, after all.

I wondered what he was gonna tell the others when I didn't show up at four forty-five.

Larry shoved me rudely, snapping me back to my present situation.

"Wait," I said, looking at the cop who'd shown me the letter. I decided he was "good cop" and Larry was "bad cop". "You just read that letter. Don't you get it? That guy, Z, he's been pissed at me. He just left me a note telling me we're even. Isn't it obvious he set me up?"

"It's obvious he owed you big-time," said Larry, who was now dragging me by the arm through the door. "Owed you something he could only pay back with a metric shit-ton of drugs. Nice of him to let you know you're even, right?"

I had to admit that was a valid interpretation . . . if you had no idea what my relationship with Z was like.

"Hey," said the third cop suddenly. "He was right. This guy isn't Jeff Stamos."

My wallet was open in his hands, and he was

examining my primary credit card. "Jason L. Jorgensen. Why you calling yourself Jeff?"

I shrugged, trying to hide my panic. "Maybe I'm calling myself Jason."

Larry'd stopped and was looking pensive, at the edge of comprehension. "Jason L. Jorgensen . . . Where've I heard that name?" He looked at me, frowning like his shitty memory was somehow *my* fault. "I swear I've seen you before."

"No license," said the other cop, shutting my wallet with a snap.

"We've never met," I said to Larry, but he kept looking at me, determined.

Good cop sucked a breath of air through his teeth. "I think I know what it is, Larry."

I waited for the blow to fall.

"Jorgensen was a name attached to that murder case a few months back. The cop shooting."

Whatever guardian angel out there had my back, I was immensely thankful for him right now.

"Hector Davis," said Larry solemnly, and the

temperature of the room suddenly felt two degrees cooler. "Best cop in the city. The Mafia needed five men to bring him down, and he was worth all of them put together."

It might've been my imagination, but I thought I saw the cop with my wallet's face freeze momentarily at the mention of the Mafia. It passed so quickly, though, I couldn't be sure.

"One of the people on-site was a Jorgensen, I think," said good cop. "Hector, his kid, and his kid's friend Jorgensen."

"That was me," I said quickly. "That's probably where you've seen me before—they took my picture a bunch of times."

Larry stared a little longer, then finally, he gave a little, placated grunt.

Thinking of Hector's death brought my thoughts back to Z and his treachery. Sure, our relationship'd been pretty rocky lately, but I'd been putting in real effort, and I'd thought things were getting better between us. Had he been playing me, pretending to soften so I'd let my guard down enough to stab me in the back?

When'd he planted the cocaine? When'd he left the *note*? He could've been facing down Lorenzo Michaelis with me in the Catskills knowing that if we escaped, a cell was waiting for me. While I stood over him in the hospital, he could've been imagining me in cuffs.

"It was the worst day of my life," I said, trying to keep wallet cop in my field of vision without making it obvious I was watching him. "I'm really grateful for how your department came together against the Mafia and cleaned up the streets."

There. Something'd definitely changed in wallet cop's expression that time. I ticked the odds of his being one of the Mafia's traitor cops up to sixty percent. There were probably ways I could use that to my advantage, but right now, I was preoccupied by how much worse his presence made the situation. I offered no resistance as Larry shut down the conversation again and started moving, tugging me along behind him. We passed through the door into the living room, then towards the entrance hallway.

And then I saw the hoodie. Still lying where I'd left it, by the front door. Right next to the two-million-dollar backpack.

I knew what'd happen if I drew attention to the hoodie. I *knew*. But if I didn't, there was a chance it'd be ID'd as Kira's. And that could potentially give *everything* away.

A chance was still too much. Even knowing that, I almost couldn't bring myself to do it.

I managed to choke the words out on the lip of the still-open apartment door. "Can I take that hoodie?"

"You won't be able to keep it," said Larry.

"Yeah, but . . . it's cold out there."

Larry looked at wallet cop. Wallet cop looked at good cop.

"No drugs or anything hidden in there, right?" said wallet cop at last.

"Uh . . . no?"

Good cop, who was still holding the comically large bag of cocaine, bent down to grab it . . . and, curious, peeked inside the still-open backpack.

I'd known it was coming, but it still felt like my heart was caught in a bear trap.

"Guys? I, uh . . . Well, you'd better take a look."

There're few things worse than getting caught with a giant bag of cocaine, but getting caught with a giant bag of cocaine *and* more than two million dollars is one of them.

Larry whistled in amazement as he looked. "That's a whole lot of cash. Can't believe we almost walked past it."

He picked up the backpack and handed it to wallet cop. "We're gonna wanna take this with us. This guy's a big deal."

I couldn't even *begin* to calculate how long my sentence'd be at this point—but given that I'd just lost my primary means of affording a lawyer, it was probably far too high.

On the bright side, at least good cop gave me the hoodie . . . after searching it thoroughly for contraband.

"This way," said Larry, dragging me out of the apartment and towards the elevators. When we got there, he jabbed a thick thumb into the down-arrow button and left it there until a soft *ding* heralded the elevator's arrival.

The doors slid open and Larry ushered me inside. Good cop and wallet cop followed him in, then good cop pressed and held the "lobby" and "door close" buttons. I guess the cops knew that trick too. Actually, it'd probably been programmed in for their convenience.

"You were a loose cannon back there, Richter," Larry scolded good cop as we started moving. "That shit with the letter. They could cite you for that shit, come *on*."

Richter looked suitably chastened, and I felt a little bad for him. He'd been at least sorta willing to gimme a chance. It wouldn't be right to punish him for that.

I was worried about the trip through the lobby, but I shouldn't have been—MSNBC'd moved on from the Biltmore explosion story and was now profiling a local businessman who was trying to open a vintage shoe store. We did draw attention as we walked in, but people were too focused on the cops to take a good look at me and say something as potentially ruinous as, "Hey, aren't you that guy who died earlier today?" We made it all the way through the giant glass revolving door without me so much as catching anyone's eye, and wallet cop looked none the wiser.

A pair of squad cars were parked outside the building. Larry pushed me towards the one on the right. "You're riding with me."

I stumbled a little from the push. "Easy there," I said, but I was so happy to've avoided being in a car with wallet cop, I was singing on the inside. My happiness was dampened a little by the fact that my arms were handcuffed behind my back, someone I'd thought was a friend had betrayed me, and I was about to miss a flight that literally held my life in the balance, but hey, minor victories. I'd take what I could get.

And I'd better not be too picky, because I had a feeling even minor victories'd be pretty rare for the foreseeable future.

KIRA

SOMETHING YOU GOTTA KNOW ABOUT ME IS, I'M A
survivor.

I'll take anything you throw at me and come
out on top. Someone three times my weight tried
to kill me in the ring and they had to carry him
out in a body bag. I was back on my feet in days.
My fingers still don't bend quite right. I can feel
itching inside me everywhere I'm trying to heal,
like I swallowed a colony of ants and they're scout-
ing for a home. It was so bad a couple days back, I
woke up and barfed for a half-hour straight. I said

I was taking a dump. Sometimes it gets so bad I wanna claw myself apart.

I don't, though. Because I'm a survivor.

I was ambushed by four vans packed to the gills with mobsters. They kept a steady stream of fire on my car for well over a half-hour. The car was undrivable by the time they were done, but I lost them, no problem.

I came outta that with some shrapnel injuries, nothing else. That's what being a survivor's all about.

I've got principles, but if it comes down to survival, they're gone. I tried explaining this to Z once and he said that meant I didn't have any. That little bitch. I still can't believe he's into me.

What I'm trying to say is, I love my family more than anything else in the world. I'd tear apart the entire Mafia bare-handed to keep them safe. I did my best to keep their world outta mine, just to make sure they'd be okay.

Well, *mostly* to make sure they'd be okay. There's the other reason too, which you can probably guess.

Take my love, though, and pit it against my survival? Fuck, that's not even a competition and I'm not afraid to admit it. I *can* leave my family behind. I *can* never see them again. All so I can live another day.

But that instinctive, animal part of my brain that keeps me alive said I could trust my parents with the knowledge that I wasn't actually dead. All I had to do was explain it had to stay a secret, they'd understand. It'd be enough for them to know. I was their bright star, their Kira-doll, and they didn't understand that if I was actually caught in an exploding hotel, I could shrug off that shit like Z's overly-friendly arm. I could basically *see* Dad getting thinner and thinner as he wasted away from grieving, Emma withdrawing into herself without her big sister to bring her out of her moods. And Anays wouldn't *understand* where I'd gone, would wonder loudly at the dinner table until Emma got up and left, and Mom's knuckles were white around her spoon.

I couldn't put them through that.

I parked my van across the street. Jason was worried the Mafia might still be watching the houses, if the news hadn't made it down the chain yet or something. He'd said to be careful before we left. Cautious little twerp. "Don't be careful" was basically my motto. If any goons were lurking around, they could take their best shot at me.

Their fucking funeral.

I was sorta disappointed when nobody challenged me as I crossed the street. No shouts, no sudden gunshots, no *nothing*. I guess they were gone.

The front door'd be locked, so I lifted the latch on the side gate and pushed it open. The screen door on the back porch led directly into the kitchen, and that was usually unlocked. Mom and Dad were at work and Emma and Anays were in school. I was counting on that, because saying bye face to face'd be too tough. I might even *cry*, and I don't remember the last time I cried. Nobody deserved to sit through that kind of weepfest, least of all my parents. Much better to leave a note.

Though now that I thought about it, they could've been sent home from work early given the circumstances . . .

I was suddenly a whole lot tenser than before. But I wasn't gonna stop now just because my parents might be home. Maybe I'd bawl a bit if they showed, but it'd "have no significant effect upon the success rate of the plan," as Jason might say. By that I mean they wouldn't convince me to stay behind or anything like that. There's too much of the survivor in me.

I was hoping I'd run into Jasmine, our pissy kitty, on my way through the yard, but she was probably hiding again. Jasmine stuck around because we fed her, but it's not like she *liked* us. She's the only cat I ever met that didn't like to be petted. But she was a fighter, like me, so I respected her a bit even if she didn't return the favor. You can't expect cats to respect you. That's just not something they do.

Whatever. She wouldn't understand goodbyes, she was just a cat. She wouldn't even notice I was gone, I bet. And if she did, she'd probably be happy, that asshole cat.

The screen door stuck slightly as usual. It always pissed me off before, but now it seemed like a good-natured quirk of the house. I couldn't imagine living somewhere that *didn't* have a sticky screen door. I'd grown up with that door, lived through all the attempts to fix it. It meant something to me somehow, besides shitty engineering.

Once the door was open, I stepped inside and listened. The fat load of nothing I heard convinced me the house was like I'd expected it to be, empty. Good.

The kitchen table'd be a good place to put my letter, or maybe on the island, by the sink. They were both equally noticeable. In the end, the idea of putting it next to a sink turned me off of the island, so I wiped off the kitchen table with a sponge and dried it with my shirt.

I wasn't proud of the letter, but it'd get the job done and I'd spent too long puzzling over it at this point. It was as ready as it was ever gonna be.

Mom and Dad,

I just want to let you know I'm safe and alive. Don't believe the news. We set it up that way because people were trying to kill us and we needed them to think we were dead. Don't worry, it worked for now, but we need to leave the country before they figure things out. It's probably safer if I don't tell you where exactly. I know it sucks but you have to pretend like I died still, so nobody catches on. Even once I'm gone. Wherever we go, they can follow.

There's a lot of stuff you don't know about me. I'm sorry for that. I got mixed up in some stuff I can't tell you about. It's not your fault or anything. You were great parents.

Please don't tell anyone I'm alive. I wasn't supposed to tell <u>anyone</u> in the first place but I *couldn't stand you worrying. The more people know, the bigger chance someone hears who shouldn't. Hopefully it'll be safe for me to come home at some point. I promise I'll come visit when I feel like I can. I hope you're not too mad at me when I do.*

I love you all,
Kira

PS: This is going to sound really weird, but I have a horse at Riverside Stables. Please take good care of him for me while I'm gone. His name is Summer Disaster and he loves racing. If you ask to talk to Frank, he'll tell you everything you need to know. He's a really sweet horse and I know Emma will love him.

PPS: I just realized you might think this is a bad prank or something. I promise it isn't.

I felt like it should be longer.

I stuck a corner under the table's empty ceramic

fruit bowl so nothing'd knock it onto the floor, but the envelope, and the words *FOR MOM AND DAD,* still showed.

The other letter, the longer one, felt heavy in my pocket and I drew it out as well, wondering if I should put it with the first. Maybe under or something. But when I moved to put it on the table, my hand refused to open.

I didn't wanna leave this one.

But I *had* to. It was my last chance to come clean, own up to everything. The bloodlust, the crimes, the murders. It was a pretty exhaustive list of all the shit I'd kept from my family over the years. Stuff they couldn't know while I was alive.

I dunno how long I stared at that envelope. Long enough that the words on it, *OPEN IN THE EVENT OF MY ACTUAL DEATH*, stayed floating in front of my eyes even while they were closed.

I was so intensely focused on that letter, I didn't notice the soft, padded footsteps until they stopped in the doorway and I realized someone was behind me. My blood iced over and my vision dulled red as I spun, letter falling to the floor as I clenched my hands into fists—

—only to relax them again as I saw that the intruder's head only barely came above my waist. It was a head I knew well, and as she recognized me, her whole face lit up in a giant smile.

"Jesus, Anays," I said as the adrenaline drained outta me, leaving a bitter, empty sort of feeling. "You scared me half to death."

"You're in *big* trouble," said Anays sternly, though her happy smile didn't even flicker. "You took the car and then didn't come home for *forever*! Daddy said he was gonna *ground* you. But we were all really scared."

She didn't know I was supposed to be dead. But that made sense, Mom and Dad were probably still trying to figure out the best way to tell her. And that reminded me.

"Aren't you supposed to be in school right now?"

"I'm sick," said Anays proudly. She coughed the phoniest cough I'd ever heard and pushed her way past me to the fridge. "I need to stay home and drink lots of orange juice 'til I get better."

Six years old and already faking sick. The kid had a bright future ahead of her, that was for sure.

And I wasn't gonna be there to see it, I realized, with a sudden lump in my throat.

"You're literally the worst, did you know that?"

Anays giggled and her proud grin widened even more. "I'm the *best*."

I picked up the letter before she could notice it. "Not what Mom said. She told me you're literally the worst and we're skipping your birthday this year."

I'm pretty sure I'd told her this *every* year, so it'd kinda lost its effect by now. Anays just scowled and turned back to the fridge, three feet of child wrapped in yellow footie pajamas.

I could've bantered with her forever, but I knew I had to go before someone else got home. The survivor in me was itching, making my muscles hum.

"I gotta go," I said reluctantly. "Tell Mom you saw me when she gets home, okay?"

"Okay!" said Anays, but her attention was fixed on the fridge.

"Bye, sis."

"Bye-bye!"

That was it, then. I turned to go. It was better she was distracted. Wasn't asking any questions I couldn't answer.

The room must've been super dusty because my eyes were stinging. I couldn't leave my kid sister like that, I'd been stupid to think I could. I turned back around to find her holding a carton of orange juice almost as big as her torso. She was hugging it to her chest with both arms.

"Can you get me a glass?"

"What's the magic word?" I said, habit forming the words before I could think twice.

"*Pleeeeease.*"

I pulled a glass off the shelf above the sink and handed it to her. She glowed as she took it in her tiny hands, clearly imagining how much juice it'd hold.

"I—" My voice caught. Like I'd caught bitch-disease. "I'm gonna miss you, you know that?"

I guess she noticed something in my voice because she looked up sharply from the cup at that, with sudden seriousness. Her big eyes were fixed on my face, reading me. She saw something there. Maybe everything. And she *understood.*

"I gotta go," I said again, forcing the words through my clogged throat. Jesus. I sounded like a squashed raccoon. And if I didn't get outta this house now, I wouldn't be able to leave.

Anays nodded solemnly. "Huggles?" she asked.

She sounded so sincere, like she could solve all the world's problems by hugging them. But you can't, because real life isn't Bollywood. Fuck if it wasn't the cutest thing I'd ever seen though, my kid sister standing next to a carton of OJ with her arms outstretched and her face deadly serious.

I pulled her into a tight hug and lifted her off

the ground. She gave as good as she got, squeezing me so hard I swear I heard something crack. Not that that was hard to do, given the shape my body was in right now.

"Be good," I said. I put her down, but she wouldn't let go, clinging like a limpet around my back. Slowly, painstakingly, I peeled her off, even if my heart broke while I did it. Jesus Christ, I loved her so much and I was never gonna see her again.

"See you later," I lied, and then I power-walked outta there before I lost the will to leave.

I was almost to the front door when I remembered the second letter, still in my hand. I stood rooted to the carpet for a few seconds, staring at it.

Anays deserved to grow up thinking of her sis as the cheery mama's-girl I'd pretended to be, not who the letter showed me as. I'd been trying to get rid of that person most of my life. I could at least let the truth die with me, leave her behind in death. Be remembered as the girl I'd always wished I was.

The paper gave easily beneath my fingers as I tore at it, rent it like skin until it was a couple hundred tiny pieces and completely unreadable. Then I balled them together into a crumpled mass in my fist.

I tossed them into a random recycling bin as I left.

ADDIE

I MOVED UP THE FRONT STEPS OF MY HOUSE AND MY bubble of sound moved with me. It was always a transparent blue in my mind, though quite invisible in reality—I couldn't actually *see* it, but it was so obviously present that my sight couldn't help but conjure it up. It was a soft, flickering presence around me, expanding as my feet hit the concrete and contracting just as quickly as the sound died away.

It was an unrealistic depiction of sound at best,

but a useful one. If I kept the bubble away from people, kept it small enough that nobody else occupied its space, I probably couldn't be heard. Obviously not foolproof—some people had more sensitive hearing than others, and approximating that was mostly guesswork—but close enough.

Currently, the bubble wasn't in danger of touching anybody. There weren't many people on the street right now—the closest was tending his ferns approximately forty meters to my left—and those who *were* had more important things to do than people-watch. I probably hadn't needed my disguise, but nobody ever got shot being *too* safe—also, it wouldn't do for a friendly neighbor to notice my continued existence. As it was, anyone who looked my way would see the dark blouse and clipboard tucked under my arm, silently pity Ms. Mendez, and hope their house wasn't on my list. There was no indication of *what* exactly I was inspecting, but that hardly mattered. Inspections are bad news. Everyone knows that.

The hinges on the door had been squeaking when I left for the Catskills a week and a half ago, and that's not the sort of thing *Mamá* would be attentive to. Thankfully, I'd done some experimenting and determined that you could mitigate the problem by applying upward pressure to the knob as you turned. My bubble still expanded dangerously as I opened the door, but manageably so, and it receded as the tiny squeak died away. I left the door open behind me—even if the first noise had gone unheard, a second might not. Something as blatant as an opened door will often be explained away by a person's subconscious, while the smallest innocuous noise garners suspicion. Humans are funny that way.

I put the clipboard on the dining room table as I passed through. It was stacked high with papers of all kinds, and I couldn't remember the last time we had actually eaten on it. Most of our meals were taken in the kitchen, standing up against the stove. I'd offered to organize the papers and clean it more than once, but *Mamá* always shook her head no.

Speaking of the kitchen, I heard low voices as I approached it. This was anomalous—*Mamá* didn't get many visitors, and while she talked to herself sometimes, it was usually while playing poker online, which she did from the comfort of her bedroom. The only people who tended to visit her were debt collectors, and they were rarely this subdued.

It could be a *calm* debt collector . . . but a few seconds with my ear against the door invalidated that theory, thankfully. No, *Mamá* actually had a guest over for once. The thought of her making a friend touched my heart briefly, before I listened to the conversation a little longer and realized they were discussing *me*.

In hindsight, I should have predicted that people might stop by to offer their condolences. But in my defense, it's hard to visualize a world you're absent from, for obvious reasons. The idea that there was a community actively reacting to my death was difficult to conceptualize, seeing as how I was still alive.

When their conversation started winding down, I slipped under the dining room table, far back enough to cut off the sightlines of all but the shortest of people. Then I waited ten minutes or so for them to *actually* finish before finally, the kitchen door opened. Through it walked a pair of sensible flats attached to a skinny pair of dark legs.

I zeroed in on them, selected reference points, and pattern-matched through my memory until I came up with the name and face those legs belonged to. Jessica Davis, Z's mother.

It twisted my gut to imagine *Mamá* and Mrs. Davis consoling each other in our kitchen, trying to make sense of the shortness of their children's' lives. Imagining *Mamá's* grief never failed to evoke an emotional response. Imagining Mrs. Davis's barely affected me at all. Even when I realized that by coming here, Mrs. Davis would miss her chance to see her son.

I imagined Z arriving at his house and finding it empty. That wasn't enough either, even though Z was my friend. So instead of revealing myself and telling Mrs. Davis her son was still alive, I crouched motionless and hidden from view, taking breaths so shallow my bubble of sound didn't even scrape the tabletop, until I heard the front door open and close again. Then I slid forward on the balls of my feet, stood, took five soundless steps forward, prepared myself mentally, and pushed open the kitchen door.

She was sitting on a stool by the dishwasher with her back to me, shoulders hunched in sadness.

"*Mamá,*" I said softly. "I'm home."

She jerked her head around so fast it almost gave *me* whiplash, saw me, and went deathly pale.

There was a long, awkward silence.

"Sorry I worried you," I said.

"*Worried* me?" she said. "All the news has been repeating is that you . . . "

Her face was awash with confusion, but as I watched, it transitioned slowly to relief . . . and then, even more quickly, to anger.

"Is this your idea of a *joke*? Make your *pobre* mother sick with sadness and then sneak into the house without knocking and tell me you're home like you've been out shopping?"

I *never* knock, and she knows it. But now didn't seem like a good time to point that out.

"I didn't have a choice—" I began, but she swept me into her arms, cutting me off. She was crying freely now, all the tears she hadn't let herself cry before. I felt a sudden surge of tenderness, which was good, because it meant my emotions weren't completely dead yet.

Sometimes I go so long without feeling anything that it's hard to tell.

Eventually, the flood subsided and I decided to take control of the conversation. "*Mamá*," I said firmly, disengaging and putting her at arm's length. "I'm here to say goodbye."

And then I told her everything.

It wasn't easy. When you spend as much of your life as I do hiding, it's hard to let the barriers down. But it came out, in pauses and stutters and vagaries that bore little resemblance to my usual composure.

And *Mamá* listened. She didn't always do the best job hiding her shock, or (at times) her disapproval, but it's not every day you discover your daughter's a petty thief. Or a con artist. Or an accessory to murder. Or any of a dozen other things.

When I finished, her eyes were sparkling with new tears. Her mouth opened, then closed again under the weight of everything it wanted to say.

"It's been a rough year," I said at last.

"*Evidentamente.*"

Another, longer silence, during which *Mamá* seemed to draw into herself.

"*Lo siento*," she said, resting a small hand on my cheek. "For the way I have lived. The example I have set. There is no room in my heart for blame. How could there be, when all of it lies at my feet?"

"It's not like that."

"You would not see it that way," she sighed. "But if I had not been in debt, would you have stolen for me? If you'd had a *padre* to look up to, would you—"

"I made my own choices," I said, trying to keep the edge out of my voice. "This is who I am. It's not your fault."

That only made her look sadder. I could feel my own face hardening into the neutral mask I often wore, a reflex associated with emotional dis-comfort. I had to fight to keep it relaxed.

From her perspective, it would seem that I'd been stealing for her sake—that's even the story I told myself, in the beginning. That because I was giving her the money I took, that made it selfless.

But no. I'd stolen because it felt right to

me—because I was at *home* avoiding sight lines and circumventing security systems. It had certainly never been about the money—otherwise, it wouldn't have been so easy to hand over, time after time. Sure, I'd been worried for her—deathly so on some occasions—but that worry had been as much excuse as call to action.

And for the people I stole from, I couldn't bring myself to care. They were shadows to me, constructions of vapor in a world I alone inhabited. Caring about them was just so *wearying*. It drained me if I tried, and I never could maintain it for long . . . so why try? I hadn't even cared for Jason at first, not even when I'd kissed him. It had just sort of *happened* over time, and against my better judgment. Now I wouldn't do without those feelings for all the gold in Fort Knox. They represented the possibility that I *could* learn to feel again. If I could do it for one person, I could do it for everyone. And that was the most valuable thing anyone had ever given me—except the gift of life from *Mamá*, of course. And now that I no longer needed to fake my feelings for him, he'd never need to learn what had actually motivated that first kiss.

I've always been good at keeping secrets.

"Speaking of which, this is for you," I said, reaching into my purse and pulling out several stacks of bills. "Just in case you get into trouble. Don't worry, I didn't steal it. It's bounty money. What the Mafia paid the man who killed us."

I had no reason to keep it—I would have given her the entirety of my share, but I'd only been able to fit so much in my purse. If I needed more, I had my own ways of obtaining it. *Mamá* didn't.

Mamá didn't take the money, so I put it on the kitchen table. "You can't gamble with it," I said sternly. "It's for emergencies."

"*No puedo tomarlo*," she protested, but I stood my ground.

"It's just money, *Mamá*. It's not tainted or anything."

She didn't look convinced, but she dropped the subject, faster than I'd expected her to—I'd been prepared for an argument. Instead, she'd offered a token resistance and folded as soon as I insisted. As if she actually *needed* it . . .

"*Mamá*, do you owe money again?"

I tried to meet her eyes, but she looked anywhere but my face—which told me all I needed to know. But I pretended her evasion had worked. There was nothing to gain from further confrontation. I was just glad I'd had money to give her—and I'd wire more later if it wasn't enough.

"Never mind," I said. "It's getting late. I'm meeting the others at the airport . . . "

Mamá stiffened when I reminded her I couldn't stay. She was suddenly radiating worry from every pore in her body. Her every motion was screaming it so loudly that even *Kira* would have picked up on it. "You don't have to go," she said, but the words felt wrong, like she'd realized how false they were as she said them.

"My flight's leaving in a couple hours," I said, arranging my face into an approximation of the conflict I didn't feel. But *Mamá* would see that false conflict and be mollified, somewhat, that the decision had at least been difficult. Sure enough, the lines in her face smoothed slightly.

People are like books. You have to invest effort into reading them carefully, but often a glance at the front is all you need to approximate the rest. The gang always said I was good at reading people, and they weren't wrong, but I don't actually read people too often—it takes too long.

I *extrapolate.*

I extrapolated her next move a second too late, as she was making it. Her eyes narrowed and her cheeks stiffened in determination as she pulled her cellphone out of her pocket and tapped it rapidly. She was holding the screen towards herself but I didn't need to see it to know what number she'd just dialed. There aren't too many people you can reach with only three digits.

"Stay," she said. "Or I'll go to the *policía*."

"Tell anyone and I'll be dead before I leave the country."

I met her gaze, let the truth of my words resonate from my eyes to hers. I knew her threat for what it was—the final desperate bluff of a mother losing her child—and that she would never actually follow through.

"Your friends are dangerous." Her hand was still on that *call* button. "*Van a hacer que te maten*, Addison. Do you know what your friend Kira *did* in that living room? Do you?"

"No," I said truthfully. But I could imagine all too well. Ever since Jason had realized the truth about what had happened the night Kira saved *Mamá*, I'd been picturing it. And I have a *very* active imagination.

But seeing the revulsion on *Mamá*'s face made me wonder just which details we were missing.

"They're good people," I said evenly, still maintaining eye contact. "I'll be safe with them. But if you call the police, the Mafia *will* know I'm alive. Not even prison will keep them from me."

Slowly, haltingly, she lowered the phone.

"*Te amo, Mamá,*" I said, projecting warmth into my words.

I watched the internal battle play out over her face, and saw the exact moment resignation won.

"*Te amo, hermosita,*" she whispered through white lips.

To my surprise, I felt my eyes prickling a little. It had been years since she called me that.

But not even all the pet names in the universe could keep me from making my plane. I gave *Mamá* a large hug, promised I'd be safe, apologized a couple dozen times, the works. Somewhere in there, she started crying again. I gave her as much time as I thought I could afford, then extricated myself.

Back through the dining room, past the table piled high with paper, across the living room to the door. For the last time. If I had left time to linger, I would have wandered the halls until every last picture frame was etched into my memory. I would have stared at the exterior until I could form a snapshot in my mind.

Instead, I took a quick glance over my shoulder as I walked back down the street towards the bus station, clipboard in hand.

How anticlimactic.

There was only one more errand—picking up our new passports—before I could make my way to LaGuardia. I wondered how Jason was getting on. He probably wasn't saying bye to his dad, but he wouldn't want to waste his last hours in New York either. I sent off a quick text.

said bye. It suckd. What r u up2?

I waited a few seconds, but I got no reply. Probably in the middle of something important, then. I tried to come up with a list of important things Jason would do without telling me, and came up with exactly *one*. But I trusted him too much to even *consider* that explanation—there could be a dozen reasons he wasn't texting me back. His phone could be out of battery, for example.

It wasn't that big a deal. I would see him at the airport in a few hours either way. We could talk then.

2

I'D STAYED ON-SITE LONG ENOUGH TO SEE JASON being led outta the apartment in cuffs. I had to be sure. It would've been just like him to talk (or buy) his way outta trouble. But I relaxed when I saw Larry Burgess leading him. Burgess was one of that rare breed, a trustworthy cop. Dad used to tell stories about him, before he . . .

Anyway, Burgess'd been offered bribes before. Once, a perp tried bribing a squad he was on. Burgess refused the bribe, then busted the other cops for accepting. After that, nobody tried to bribe Officer Burgess no more.

Not the most popular guy on the force, in

other words. But damned if they weren't lucky to have him.

I'd kinda wanted to follow him to the station, just to be sure. Jason could pull a plan outta his ass in a car ride's time, no problem, and he could work fucking *miracles* sometimes. I'm big enough to admit that. But he'd been nice enough to schedule me a flight outta LaGuardia to Copenhagen, and I intended to make it before someone recognized me and had me shot. Not going through that again. Once was enough.

And here I was, at LaGuardia Airport, and Jason was still nowhere to be seen. What could he even *do* to escape in this situation? Nothing came to mind, just a confused jumble. That's why I'd let him make the plans for this long. I suck at it. It took my whole hospital stay to work this one out. But it was worth it just to imagine how Jason must feel having a plan crash down around *his* head for once, instead of mine.

I don't wanna come off as bitter, and I can

excuse a bit of random chance screwing me over. But not the eighth or ninth fucking time. Seems like every plan he made, Z ended up fucked. So why not take matters into my own hands and make sure it was *him* this time?

"You okay, dude? You're zoning out again."

I blinked. Kira was waving a hand in front of my face.

"Yeah, I'm good," I said. "I'll be better when we're on this plane."

"I feel that."

Kira'd already been here when I showed up. I wonder how long her goodbyes must've taken to be shorter than mine, which hadn't happened. I'd needed to be on-site at Jason's apartment to coordinate things so the cops showed while he was there, or the timing never would've worked. When I'd realized that, I'd almost called everything off. I wanted to see Mom so bad. I wanted to give her that peace of mind. But I couldn't let Jason keep screwing my life the way he had.

Hopefully, God would understand why I'd made the choice I had.

Plus, it's not like my family were the only people I'd abandoned without a trace. There were hundreds of people in New York alone I couldn't say "bye" to because it might blow our cover. Good friends, people I cared about. And I had to hurt all of them by being dead because Jason'd decided that was the best plan and plowed ahead because *he* couldn't see anything wrong with that. And why would he? Pretty much everyone he gave a shit about was coming with him.

I was leaving my entire fucking *life* behind. And he didn't care. Somehow, that'd been enough to move me to action when not even using Dad's death like he'd done had. On that day, my trust in Jason'd been broken forever. And now, today, I'd finally really done something about that broken trust.

I'd tried stepping back. They'd brought me back in.

I'd tried getting revenge by myself. They'd found out about it and made it their own.

I'd tried to forgive Jason for all the shit he'd pulled. And then he'd uprooted our entire lives without even caring.

"What time is it?" I asked Kira. It couldn't be long before the rendezvous time now, and there was no sign of a miraculously-escaped Jason. But I wouldn't be sure I'd actually gotten rid of him until the plane was in the air without him on it.

Kira pointed at a giant clock on the wall, which flashed *4:43* in blocky red numbers. "Next time, don't ask stupid questions."

Four minutes.

"You think the others'll show?"

"Sure," I said. "Why wouldn't they?"

"I guess," said Kira. And that's when I realized I'd fucked up.

Even if *Jason* didn't make it, Addie would. By itself, this wasn't a problem, I have some issues with Addie but nothing major. But here's the thing—Addie was the queen of reading people.

Of course she'd fucking ask about Jason. The two were pretty much Siamese twins. And the moment she did, my face'd give everything away.

The airport suddenly seemed very warm and crowded.

"I, I gotta use the bathroom," I managed to stammer, and Kira shrugged as if to say, "Sure, why bother telling *me*?" Thanking God for how oblivious she was, I stumbled away to splash some water on my face and get ahold of myself. Addie wasn't perfect. I could fool her.

It took some serious concentration remembering to avoid eye contact with the people I passed. Head low, posture slumped. If a friend recognized me, it could be trouble. I'd had to bite back a few instinctive *hi*'s already. But I made it to the bathroom without anyone I knew calling me over.

I took a sec to glance in the mirror. My cheeks were still pretty wet from the water, so I wiped them on my shirt. Then I started practicing my innocent face. It sucked. But my hair looked good, at least. I patted it, which was soothing.

I make a big deal outta my hair but that's just because it's the only part of my head I like. Gotta show off your strengths, right? Only I wish the rest of me would pull its weight.

I came outta the bathroom feeling a little better, determined to just act natural. Addie'd arrived in the time I spent steeling myself, and she was already speaking urgently to Kira. I could guess what she was talking about, and when I got in hearing range, I knew my guess was right.

" . . . *never* late. And if something delays him, he texts."

Addie's a cool human being, if a bit off-putting. Nothing big, just sometimes she messes up at pretending her feelings and I remember she's consciously constructing her empathic responses. Not gonna lie, that scares me a little, especially since I can't understand it at all, but at least she's good enough at it most of the time that I can pretend she's normal. But when I see her all cuddled up with Jason, I think about how easy they had it finding each other, and then the clusterfuck that's me and Kira, and it makes me too jealous to stand. I used to look at them and hope Kira'd notice we were always third and fourth wheeling and decide maybe we should solve that for both of us and get together.

That girl drives me crazy. She's got this *aura* that never fails to draw my gaze. And recently, she's been pretty into me. But that kinda sucks because *recently*'s also when I discovered she'd become a psychopath.

Just another reason Jason's the biggest asshole to ever walk the planet. See, Kira was always a little insane. Not in a bad way or anything, she obviously had some issues she was hiding. But Jason never cared about that. He saw someone who was willing to get physical and thought, *Great, now how can I use that?* He never once thought that maybe he shouldn't be encouraging her. But he pushed her further and further, and she got worse and worse until *he* got scared of her. *That's* when he decided there was a problem, but it was already way too late for the girl I used to know, the one with the carefree laugh and the sharp tongue. There was just this crazy, abrasive berserker he'd created to fight his battles for him.

Now I don't really know where I stand with Kira, other than "not in her way." All the attraction's still there, but I'm also scared to death she might literally kill me. You know, your average teenage romantic worries.

"I turned my phone back on just in case. Nothing."

"I'm back," I announced. "Hi Addie. 'Sup?"

"Jason isn't here yet," she said. Which I *guess* answered the question, though not very politely. She shoved my new passport and ID (my new *identity*) into my hands. Kira was already holding hers.

"Well, it's only four forty-nine," I pointed

out, looking over at the clock Kira'd pointed out. "Maybe he's running late."

"That's what *she* said," said Addie, and Kira let out a hearty guffaw.

"I thought I was the only one who made those."

"I didn't—dammit, this is *serious.*"

"Let's give it ten more minutes," I suggested, picking as big a number as I thought I could get away with and praying to God he wouldn't show up before then. Or at all.

Ten minutes later, Jason still hadn't miraculously arrived and I was having trouble keeping a triumphant smile off my face. Addie was pacing so tightly she was wearing a pattern in the carpet.

"I just had a thought," I said. "Jason thinks his family's a bunch of fuckheads. Maybe he got here way earlier than us and already went through security."

"Without his passport?" said Addie acidly. "I've got his right here. He could hardly use his *own.*"

I gave her what I hoped was a confident stare.

"We're talking about the guy who carries two phones around just in case he gets mugged. I'm *sure* he has like five backup identities."

She wasn't buying it.

"Even if he isn't there, he has the gate info. So he can find us no problem. But I think he is. It's just like him to go on ahead."

That genuine bitterness at the end sold it, I think. Addie's already-shadowed face darkened, but she didn't call me on my lie.

"Let's go, then."

We weren't bringing enough luggage to check a bag, but we did anyway, because it was the only way to get our cash through security without raising awkward questions. Just one bag, with our three shares carefully separated by a bunch of random shit for padding. Hopefully, it'd all still be there on the other side. At Addie's suggestion, we took a few hundreds each and slid them into our wallets, just in case. I thought we should take a bit more, but Addie didn't want us pushing our luck.

We were halfway to security when I realized she was already positioning herself as team leader. She'd framed our argument that way without me even noticing, and if *I* hadn't noticed, it was pretty much a given that Kira hadn't either. But Kira didn't really care about that shit. She'd follow orders if she felt like it, and wouldn't if she didn't. Who gave them didn't mean crap.

I didn't really care if Addie was team leader. She was probably the best one for the job. I just didn't like how she'd *assumed* it.

We passed through security easily, since none of us had carry-ons. I'd been worried about whether being legally dead would keep us from getting through, but the agents just looked at our fake IDs and waved us on. I guess there wouldn't be much point in canceling dead peoples' tickets.

"That shit is so *pointless*," Addie seethed in just above a whisper after we passed through. "Security theatre, and not even convincing at that. I could get whatever I wanted through there."

"Yeah?" I pretended to be interested. Anything to keep her talking about something else. "Where're the weak spots?"

"That backscatter scanner, for starters. It's really easy to fool . . . "

She didn't stop talking until we reached the gate. I nodded in all the right places and kept my eyes wide, hoping I could keep the conversation going, but she clammed up as soon as she'd swept the waiting area and not seen Jason.

"Not here," she said.

"He'll show up."

Now her eyes were glinting suspiciously, but she didn't say anything.

Addie's pacing grew more and more pronounced as the minutes ticked by. She tried several times to engage Kira and me in conversation about where Jason could be, but backed off when we made it clear the answer was, "We dunno." I imagined Jason in a similar position at the police station, looking at the clock, knowing he was gonna miss the plane, begging to use a phone. It almost made me feel bad, and I'd told myself I wasn't *gonna* let myself feel bad. Jason was rich enough to afford the best lawyer money could buy, and still have enough to post his own bail ten times over. He wouldn't be in the slammer for long. Just long enough to lose track of us, so we could slip away and start a life that wasn't in danger of being fucked up by him. I already had plans to get us outta Copenhagen to make things that much harder for him.

And then? Maybe things could finally turn around for Kira and me. Without *him* around, without us fighting for our lives, maybe she'd mellow out a bit. Go back to being the old Kira. And then . . . well, she already liked me, I was pretty sure. She'd been giving me some serious signals for the past couple months.

Two rich teens and an entire beautiful continent to explore. Anything could happen. Anything at all.

"Good afternoon, passengers. This is the

pre-boarding announcement for Virgin Atlantic flight fourteen twenty-four to Copenhagen. We are now inviting those passengers with small children, and any passengers requiring special assistance, to begin boarding at this time. Please have your boarding pass and identification ready. Regular boarding will begin in approximately ten minutes' time. Thank you."

The announcement cut off in a burst of static. Addie was stiff as a starched-up shirt. Her eyes closed and did not immediately reopen.

"Jason's still not here," said Kira.

"*I know!*" snapped Addie with such fire that people looked at her. She took a breath. "Something's happened to him."

"The Mafia," I said grimly, and Addie's face took on the masklike quality that on her indicates strong feelings.

I laid a consoling hand on her shoulder and she shrugged it away fiercely. "No. He's not dead. I'd *know* if he was. I know that sounds stupid, but I would."

Kira and I looked bemusedly at each other but didn't say anything. If Addie noticed, she ignored us.

"He might need us," she said quietly.

I let the full extent of my disbelief show. Genuine disbelief, for how stupid she was being. "Seriously? No. No. No. We have a *plan*."

"But Jason didn't know this would happen when he made it," said Addie. Her conviction was building. "We can't leave without him. Not before we know what went wrong."

"He'd do the same for us," Kira echoed.

My plan, my beautiful plan, was dissolving around me, caving in like a rock hut in an earthquake. I felt like hitting something again. But that probably wouldn't go over well in an airport.

"No," I said firmly. "We are getting on that plane. You know how bad the mob wants us dead? The longer we stay, the bigger the chance of us blowing our cover! We're lucky nobody's recognized me yet, but if we stroll back through this airport . . ."

Addie squared her shoulders and faced me. A challenge. "We are *not* leaving without Jason."

When Addie turns the full force of her intensity on you, it's hard to remember how short she is. I've got two inches on her and she was towering over me.

I shook my head. "Great. This is so familiar, I can tell y'all right now how it shakes out. Jason's missing as part of some super-convoluted plot he didn't tell any of us about. We panic and stay off the plane. Someone recognizes me, spreads the word I'm not dead, it gets back to the mob, and they shoot me. You guys too, maybe, but *definitely* me. Because whenever a plan goes tits up, I'm the one who gets fucked. But not this time. This time, I'm playing it safe."

I was trying to play on their sympathy, remind them how badly Jason's plans'd always gone for me. But Addie didn't look sympathetic in the slightest.

"Fine. Play it safe. But I'm staying. Bye, Z."

"Hold up a sec," said Kira. "How'll you find us again?"

Addie hesitated, but her expression was as unreadable as ever. "Guess I won't."

I was more okay with that than I think either of them suspected. Every second Addie was around me was another second I could give something away by accident. Besides, with her gone, it really *would* be just me and Kira.

How perfect would that be?

"C'mon, A," said Kira. "We're a team. We can't split forever over this. That's not right."

"How will *Jason* find us?"

"You're here. He isn't."

"C'mon," I added. "He had his chance."

Addie slowly turned to look at me. "Alright. What aren't you telling us?"

"Huh?" said Kira.

I froze up. Of all the things she could've said, I wasn't expecting *that*. Not like I'd said anything incriminating. I couldn't even tell when she'd first noticed.

"I, uh." Addie's glare wasn't making it any easier

to think. My hands and pits were starting to sweat. "I'll tell you later."

"You'll tell us *now*."

I shook my head *no*. Not like they could make me. Kira could probably beat it out of me, but security'd step in the second she tried. I could tell she wanted to, though. Somehow, that didn't make her any less hot.

"Good afternoon, passengers. Boarding is about to begin . . . "

"Tell me," growled Addie, "or I swear I will track you down wherever you hide. And whatever it is you were keeping from us, I will punish you for it."

She put her hands on my shoulders and stared me down. Our faces were less than two inches apart. I could see every detail of Addie's face closer than I ever had before. And there was grim determination in every line on her face, and cold fire in her green eyes, and I knew when she discovered what I'd done, whatever she did to me'd make me regret it for the rest of my life.

I dunno how Jason'd never realized how *terrifying* someone who doesn't feel empathy is. I could never date someone like Addie, someone who by virtue of who she was *couldn't* care about me. Because there's no checks on what they're capable of besides what they decide. She was beyond pretending she gave the slightest shit what happened to me, and she let it show on her face for the first time. That face didn't belong on a girl just outta high school, but it would've looked perfect on an inmate at a max-security prison. And it chilled me to the core.

Here I'd thought *Kira's* anger was scary.

"Alright, okay," I managed to squeak. "I'll tell."

Addie stepped back. Her expression hadn't changed, but it wasn't scary anymore. Not sure how that worked.

I took a deep breath. "I know where Jason is. He ain't dead, or in danger."

Now that Addie's attention was focused on me,

I had to be *really* careful with my lies, and just tell the truth as much as I could.

"Then where is he?"

Oh well. Hadn't expected that to work.

"I ain't supposed to say until we're on the plane," I tried.

But I'd stretched that truth so far it was technically a falsehood, and Addie caught it immediately. "You fucking liar."

I dropped the act. "Alright. Here's how it is. You can get on the plane and I'll tell you where he is once we take off. That's a promise, no bullshit. Or you can stay here and look for him yourself. Your call. But I'm getting on that plane, and if you try and stop me, I'll shout for security. And I know some of them personally."

I let my honesty suffuse every word I spoke. Behind us, boarding continued. Addie looked at the yawning terminal and shivered as if something'd just passed over her.

"You can always fly back if you decide you have to," I pointed out.

Kira clapped her on the back. "Let's just play his fucking game. It'll be faster."

Addie's lips were a thin, white line. But she eventually gave the smallest of nods.

"Great," I said. "Then let's go."

"Shut up, dickface," said Kira. Both women were giving me looks of pure disgust, and I hadn't even told them what I'd done yet. They didn't understand how much Jason'd taken from me . . . or from *them*, for that matter. Kira didn't even *care* what he'd done to her, probably. Instead, she fucking *idolized* him. They both did. I'd never understood that.

As we got in line behind a young couple and their kid, Addie looked at the terminal again. The indecision was back on her face, and when the line moved forward, *she* didn't.

"I have a really bad feeling about this," she said.

JEEVES

BEFORE JEEVES GOT IN THE CAR TO PICK UP JASON, he left his letter of resignation with the doorman. He knew he'd never be able to get the words out in person, and leaving someone else responsible for delivery made getting cold feet and backing out impossible.

How could he pretend at pride if he couldn't even look at himself in the mirror anymore? He'd put up with Lucas's games for almost fifteen years now. At some point, you had to say enough was enough.

He only wished it hadn't taken him so long to reach this point.

ELEVEN

'D SPRUNG FOR AN UPGRADED HOLDING CELL, AND
it was hard to imagine what my room would've
looked like if I hadn't, because it was even shit-
tier than my wildest imaginings. There was a
bench along one wall, a sink on the other, and
a little hole in one corner I decided was supposed
to be a toilet. In that very same moment, I
decided I'd let my bladder rupture before I actually used it.

By the far wall was a folded gym mat. Judging
from the dirty pillow and the ragged gray blanket,
that was meant to be my bed. Did people who

didn't buy nicer accommodations *not* get these things?

At least I didn't have company anymore. They'd stuck me in a big waiting room with upwards of thirty other people before I could be checked in. I'd tried to sit in a corner and keep my face hidden, but one guy kept coming up to me and asking if I'd smuggled in any cigarettes. He asked me at least ten times and never believed me when I told him I didn't smoke. Now, at least, I was alone, with nothing to do but wonder, for hours and hours, if the others were alright.

Well, except Z—that asshole could play Russian roulette with a fully loaded gun for all I cared. And Kira, well, she'd probably be fine no matter what. So I guess I was mostly thinking about Addie. I'd used my one call to try and warn her, but her phone'd still been off, of course—just as I'd ordered, so I could hardly blame *her* for that. What'd she thought when I hadn't shown up?

I tried to imagine what she would've done, and

felt a sudden chill as I realized. She wouldn't have boarded the plane. Despite the danger, she'd stay behind. Z and Kira wouldn't, but Addie . . . What'd she said once? *You help keep me grounded. I kind of need that right now.*

Maybe that was the premonition she'd gotten from our kiss, of things ending badly. She'd stay behind for me, and the Mafia would find and kill her.

No. That was stupid. If Addie didn't wanna be found, she wouldn't be.

But dammit, I needed to get out of this cell, and I needed to do it *hours* ago. My last try hadn't gone so well, but at least I had some prep time now. Tiredness was slowing my thoughts—it had to be three a.m. or later at this point—but maybe with a quick nap . . .

My cell door clicked, jerking me immediately into wakefulness.

I watched hungrily as it opened, narrowing in on a single goal—getting through that open door by any means necessary. I wouldn't let myself miss a single avenue of escape. Any bribe, any threat, any *promise* . . .

But I took it all back when I saw the man in the doorway, so tall he had to stoop to avoid bumping his head as he entered. It was a man I knew well . . . and yet, not at all.

"I was just trying to work out how to escape this cell," I said casually, trying not to take a step back as his *presence* swept over me, filling the room. "Now I see jail might not be that bad."

Lucas Jorgensen straightened as he cleared the doorframe. At his full height, he *towered* over me—as he did over most others. I was reminded, as always, of a wolf spider looking for prey.

My barb was more for me than for him, an attempt to reduce our relationship to the antagonism of the old days, when he hadn't yet sent agents to follow me and had mysterious dealings with my mortal enemies. The "good old days," when I hadn't had to worry about him wanting me dead.

He'd be stupid to try anything *here*, but it was hard to keep from scooting into a corner as he approached, aware as I was of my vulnerability. I had to admit I didn't *know* what Lucas really wanted . . . and that was terrifying.

But at least it wasn't hard to picture him standing in front of me.

He looked me over top-to-bottom—ignoring me like my very words were beneath his notice—and finally snorted. "That outfit isn't working for you."

I shrugged. "What can I say? Good help's hard to find these days."

I didn't mention that I agreed with him. This saggy green jumpsuit wasn't doing me any favors in the looks department, but I suppose it wouldn't be doing its job if it was. Being a convict was supposed to be *un*fashionable.

"True." Lucas's lips curled like a nocked bow,

as if at some private joke. "Competent underlings are a valuable resource. That lesson, like all my others, seems to have been wasted on you."

I allowed myself a smile of my own as I recalled Kira swerving through the New York City streets, Addie infiltrating Lorenzo Michaelis's private guard, Z—but fuck Z. Fuck him twice over, because he'd put me into a situation where I had to *listen to Lucas*.

At least his voice in my head had shut up now that the real deal was here. So I didn't have *that* distracting me.

"You have no idea how well I took that lesson to heart."

The bow stretched wider. "More than you might think. But then, you *did* discover one of your tails. You knew I was watching."

He admitted it so openly, so readily—he didn't care a bit. Well, if that's how he wanted to play it . . .

"Yeah, I knew you were watching me when I

went after Richard. And I know about your acquisition of Imperial Tech, too. Must've been a cozy alliance—he gets his revenge, and you get to rid the world of a son who wouldn't give you the respect you never deserved. But here's what—"

Lucas Jorgensen laughed.

It was one of his loud, obnoxious ones, the kind that'd just drown out everything else until it subsided. Simmering with resentment, I stopped talking and waited.

When he'd decided he'd made his contemptuous mirth clear enough, he stopped. "An alliance with *Richard Trieze?* If I wanted you dead, there'd be a dozen easier ways—you didn't seriously think I was trying to kill you, did you? The fact that you still draw breath should've been enough to disabuse you of *that* notion."

Now, Lucas is a lying bastard—he's never tried to conceal that. But I somehow *knew* he was telling the truth this time. It was the way he laughed the accusation off, like he was more offended that

I'd been dumb enough to think it than at the allegation itself. If I'd been right, he would've flat-out told me. Why would he care about hiding it?

"*Kill you*," Lucas snorted. "Why would I do something like that, when I've gone to such painstaking effort to keep you alive? I've been cleaning up your fuckups since day one, and you should be thanking me for it nonstop until my next birthday, because you've had a *whole lot of fuckups*."

Somehow, paradoxically, Lucas'd grown larger while the room shrank around me. I didn't even know what to think anymore—up was down, left was right, and Lucas'd been *helping* me. And right now, he was the sort of gleeful he always got when he was about to rip someone apart.

"You made a powerful enemy in Richard Trieze," he said. "He was determined to kill you after that poker game. I had to *buy his company* to get him to back off—make it clear that I had the power to destroy him on every level, take apart his life's work systematically until no trace of him remained, before he admitted defeat. I wasn't sure if even *that* would be enough."

"It wasn't—"

"I was *very* pleasantly surprised when you arranged his death. It was just what *I* would've done—but I didn't think you had the guts."

I'd *never* been so sure I'd made the wrong decision there.

"A pity you drained his company's coffers in the process. Imperial Tech was *not* cheaply acquired, and I was hoping its stock would at least retain its value. My bottom line suffered for that."

I dunno why he was complaining, since he still had enough money to gold-plate Chicago, but any inconvenience he suffered was *something*, I guess.

"So you *did* solve that problem, eventually. Less so your numerous run-ins with the police. Especially the day you added Addison to your entourage."

"She hates that name," I muttered, but not loudly enough for Lucas to care.

"You thought Kira could just *erase the record?* There are backups offsite, which they restore daily, not to mention the dozen-odd officers who were personally involved. You're lucky I have the NYPD in my pocket, otherwise, I never could have kept them off your back the way I did. You never would've finished high school." Lucas chuckled. "No son of mine wasn't going to finish high school."

I spread my arms. "And yet I ended up here anyway. Great parenting."

"Don't you ever get tired of being insolent?"

"How could I, when you make it so easy?"

Lucas sighed, exasperated. At least I could still get under his skin. But if I'm being honest, pissing him off wasn't my primary goal, just a bonus. I was really trying to distract myself from what I'd just learned.

Keep my focus off of the fact that Lucas'd *saved* me. Multiple times. That without *him*—the man I'd been worried wanted me killed, the man who'd made my childhood a living hell—my career would've been over before it even began.

But I couldn't follow that train of thought any further. It'd tear me apart, and right now, facing that man, I needed to be at my best.

"You can thank me for surviving your little scuffle in the Catskills, too," he said. "Derek's team doesn't work for peanuts, and a job like *that* is worth significantly more than what you'd come up with. If I hadn't already had them reporting to me—"

No. *No.*

"—They just would've refused. But they knew I'd pay them what they were worth. Especially since technically, *I* was the one paying them to begin with. You know better than to hire mercenaries with someone else's money."

I took back every nice thing I'd ever thought about Derek, but not even my anger could distract me from the magnitude of my mistakes. There was no excuse for that kind of sloppiness. None.

My every success was being dismantled in front of me, and Lucas was *reveling* in it.

"*This* arrest was unexpected," he said. "Otherwise, I would've prevented it. But no permanent harm done—I've informed them of their mistake. You'll be free to go with an unblemished record, and the NYPD will still get its annual check from the Jorgensen estate."

"I don't need your help," I spat. How superior he must feel right now with his money and connections, able to wave his hand and brush aside the law. Even his being *here*, alone with a prisoner in an unlocked room, was proof of his position. Position I didn't want or need. This was *my* problem, and I could escape it myself.

Besides, the gesture smacked of a kindness Lucas didn't possess. He wanted something, and until I figured out his angle, it wouldn't be wise to appear grateful.

"And, as it turns out, you're lucky to be here."

"You're here with me. How lucky could I be?"

Lucas's smile grew somehow more smug, and all I wanted was the chance to punch it off his face. He was looking at me like I was a perfectly ripened fruit and he was trying to decide where to bite into me first.

"Alright," I said. "You know something I don't. I get it. Skip the theatrics and just tell me."

Lucas lifted his head towards the ceiling and let out a long, dramatic sigh. So much for skipping the theatrics.

"If you'd boarded the same plane as your friends, you'd be dead right now. Like they are."

Time stopped.

"It really *is* a pity that your friend's mother paid her debts with the Mafia's money—marked, of course, as a matter of procedure. That was a little *too* suspicious for Mr. Michaelis to overlook. After that, it was just a matter of checking security footage in JFK and LaGuardia. They never had a chance."

"No."

It took me a few seconds to recognize that as my voice. I'd spoken unconsciously, a flat denial of Lucas's claim, because it simply *could not* be true—

Lucas was speaking again, but there was a roaring in my ears like I was standing next to a waterfall and I couldn't hear him.

"No," I said again, but I wasn't talking to Lucas anymore. I was talking to the world. It needed to know I had not allowed this, *did not* accept it.

Because I knew. Despite my initial reaction, I knew. I could even *see* the chain of events that would've led to it, starting with my arrest. And no amount of *no*'s could stop my mind from playing those images for me.

I was *in* the waterfall, now, not just by it, and the water was beating down onto my head, and flowing inside me and chilling my heart and lungs and ribs and stomach until they were numb.

"Addie."

"I'm sorry." Lucas looked almost fatherly for a moment. "I know you fancied her."

I glared at him, wished my hatred would strike at him from deep within me. It felt strong enough. "You don't know *shit.*"

I didn't feel like crying. The tears would come later, perhaps, when things'd sunk in. When I got lonely and realized my best friends were . . .

Gone.

I'd even cry for Z, bastard that he was. It was one thing to wish him dead and quite another to learn it'd come true.

I hadn't meant it.

"They only ever held you back," said Lucas.

I did take a swing at him then, but he caught my wrist and frowned disapprovingly. I struggled against his grip. My arm wouldn't move.

"You kept them together," he said, ignoring the fact that he was holding my arm in place. "You made mistakes, but you're still a child. It would be foolish to dismiss your potential because you flew too close to the sun. With some training, you could be a remarkable asset. You were wasted on petty crimes—I think you'll find work in my organization far more satisfying."

"Ah, yes. Intern at Jorgensen International. What a life."

I'd seen Lucas eye stains on his blazer the way he was eying me now. "I wouldn't *dream* of wasting your talents like that. I have other businesses. Businesses *far* more appealing to your interests."

The subtext was obvious, even if Lucas didn't wanna risk saying it inside a federal prison. *Illegal things.*

And he was right—that *did* make it more appealing, somehow. For a brief moment, before I remembered who I was talking to.

"Fuck off."

Lucas raised one eyebrow. "Or I suppose I could just leave you here."

So that was his game. *Work for me, and I'll let you out.*

It says something about Lucas that this was actually a tough decision. On one hand, an age-stained sink, a dirty gym mat and a literal shit-hole. On the other hand . . . Mr. Wolf Spider as a boss.

"*And* let your past catch up with you. You have no idea how many investigations I'm actively preventing right now. I can't promise that protection indefinitely. You're looking at a long list of charges, even if you get the possession one dropped. Obstruction of justice, accessory to murder, trespassing, theft, accessory to battery . . . it's a long list."

I tried to match the charges to things I'd done, but that involved thinking about the others, and *that* made me want to curl into a ball on my gym mat, only I *couldn't* because Lucas was still holding my wrist. I couldn't deal with this right now. I needed to be alone so I could stop worrying about the cracks that were forming across my surface and just let myself shatter into a million pieces for a while.

"Sounds like you haven't left me with much of a choice," I said through gritted teeth. Lucas shook his head.

I'd done this to *myself*, I realized. Four years of trying to escape Lucas's shadow, and all I'd done was hand him a dossier of blackmail material.

He had me under his finger. Forever.

"I hate you," I said suddenly. It was out before I could stop myself, but I looked Lucas right in the eye as I said it, owning my feelings. Refusing to apologize. That hate was all I had now—aside from the terrible, aching sadness—and I was gonna hold onto it.

Lucas's smile didn't even crack.

"Like mother, like son," he said. "I suppose it's to be expected. But I can work with hate. I'm familiar with it. So go on hating me, by all means. Pretend it'll accomplish something. Now, are you coming or not?"

I didn't answer. But when Lucas turned to go, I took a step towards the door.

Towards *him*.

If I stayed, my life was over. I'd have nothing but myself, and Lucas'd proven I was worth basically nothing. Everyone I cared about'd still be dead.

I had to keep living, had to turn the end of everything into a beginning. For Addie and Kira. So despite myself, I followed Lucas out of that cell, one slow step at a time, hating him and myself and the world.

"I was surprised when I heard they'd picked you up," said Lucas as we walked. "I spent all morning thinking you were dead. I was *not* happy with the watchers I'd assigned to you. The plan was well-conceived."

Right.

I'd been dead.

With everything else that'd happened, that detail'd slipped my mind.

And that was when a thought occurred to me.

We'd faked our deaths once, and by Lucas's own admission, we'd done a pretty good job. And the others would've figured out something'd gone wrong when I didn't make it to the airport. They would've had an entire plane ride to make a workable plan. And sure, *I* wouldn't have been there to solve the problem, but they had Addie, which was almost as good. And Z, too, had shown a talent for plots I hadn't anticipated—much to my own detriment. Together, they *maybe* could've figured something out.

I stopped, determined to latch onto this thought before it evaporated. How would *I* have done it, if I'd been on a plane knowing my life might be in danger once I landed?

"Something wrong?" said Lucas. He'd stopped too, now.

I hesitated. If I asked for more details, he'd know I was considering this line of thought. If they *had* somehow managed to escape, and my reasoning helped Lucas realize that, he might let that information slip to the Mafia for a quick buck. I wouldn't put it past him.

But I *needed* to know. "Where'd they die? And how?"

"They made it to a hotel, far as I heard," said Lucas. "Someone broke in and shot them. It's not important—"

But my brain was already bubbling with ideas.

"Really, you're doing this? Their bodies were found at the scene. There are *pictures*."

Pictures. Okay, you'd need fake gunshot wounds. That'd be Addie's job—disguise and makeup'd been her specialty. Long as nobody got too close, they'd be fooled. Small doses of tetrodotoxin would help sell the illusion of death, at least temporarily. Z could've had a friend capable of supplying it.

After they'd been pronounced dead publicly, they could wake up and explain the situation to whoever had their bodies, maybe enter Witness Protection. It *could* work. But you'd need the assassin to be in on it too . . .

Well, the Mafia'd put a price on our heads,

right? They could hardly object if a bounty hunter got to us before *they* did. Z could've arranged that too, no problem. Yeah, we'd already used that trick once within the past forty-eight hours, but the public aspect of the plan was just new enough to make the whole thing work. The last great plan.

It was possible. That was all I needed—something to follow up on in my own time, even if odds were I'd find nothing but dead ends. It'd likely crush me all over again when I proved myself wrong, but for now, I chose to believe.

I carried that hope with me like a candle through the halls, past checkpoint after checkpoint (which Lucas waved us through), and out the front door into the cold night air. It was the one bright point in a world that'd gone horribly, unpredictably wrong in the span of a single day, and it was probably a delusion.

Jeeves was waiting in the parking lot behind the wheel of Lucas's Porsche. The doors clicked open and I climbed in, still feeling numb all over at the ease with which an entire life could end.

But where one thing ends, another can begin. Just *stopping* wasn't an option. I'd need to carry on. Somehow.

"Good evening, Master Jorgensen," said Jeeves, handing me my backpack. "Your personal effects."

Sure enough, I found my phones, wallet, and shoes atop my folded clothing . . . and Kira's hoodie, which I found myself touching like it was a modern-day Shroud of Turin. I eased it out of the bag and held it close. I didn't give a shit about the smell anymore.

And then I realized something was missing from the bag. Or rather, more than two million somethings.

"You aren't getting that back," said Lucas with a sharklike smile as he slid in on the other side. "You wouldn't know what to do with it—it'll be put to much better use in *my* hands."

His tone told me there'd be no arguing. Oh

well—I'd started from nothing before. There'd be other fortunes. Compared to my friends, it wasn't even that big a loss.

I retrieved my wallet and opened it. It was so . . . empty. A few twenties . . . and a picture of me and Addie, smiling, on a bench.

I stared at that picture as Jeeves pulled out of the parking lot. Wondered what could've been, in a different lifetime.

If they'd pulled it off . . . *If* they'd managed to snow the Mafia, the media, and everyone in between . . . Addie'd know how dangerous dropping her cover would be. She was someone else now—not that she'd be unused to that. If she ever even *hinted* to me she was alive, it'd be against her better judgment.

And yet . . .

You help keep me grounded. I kind of need that right now.

She could be anyone, I realized, and I'd never know. A fellow pedestrian on the sidewalk. A vendor hawking bootleg DVDs in the subway. One of the many homeless people in Central Park.

Keeping an eye on me. But never breaking character.

I wouldn't put any real energy into searching for the truth, because finding something might jeopardize their safety. But I'd believe. I'd hope.

And, no matter what Lucas had in store for me, I'd *remember*.